T H A N K ʏ O U

Mum, Dad, Nina and Isobel, I thank you first. Thank you for your continued perseverance, understanding and support. Thank you for not giving up on me. Family is everything.

Lucy, you are my home. I will never truly be able to thank you for all that you have done for me.

To my friends through thick and thin, thank you for listening to me. You know who you are.

To those who are no longer in my life but have travelled with me along this journey at one stage or another... thank you.

Finally, to my A-Level English Language tutor, I thank you too. Whilst your intentions pure, your capacity to patronise and belittle has inspired me in many ways more than my own determination ever will.

Better, not bitter.
Thank you.

D I S C L A I M E R

PRE - FACE

A letter to my younger self

Dear **You**,

We did it, you miserable bastard.

I'll let the euphoria sink in for a moment longer because of course you won't have the faintest idea as to what I'm talking about. It is 2016 after all. You're so vain, you probably think this letter is about you. Well, it is. I'm sorry for the ambiguity. I'm not as witty as I think I am, but you already knew that didn't you?

Anyway, it's me, it's you. I hope my letter finds you well, please don't be as paranoid as I know you're going to be. I'm not hiding behind a lamppost under the guise of a baseball cap watching your reaction upon reading this letter for the first time, that would be ridiculous. I'm finally getting back to you; it's been six years.

Regrettably, I'm not writing to you with instruction or guidance on saving mankind from disease or disaster so let's refrain from becoming overly excited, shall we? I know how impressionable you can be.

Without confessing too much at what lies ahead, I can confirm a few suspicions. After all, what's a few clandestine sanctions between friends? Or are we family? I don't know, I've never done this before.

Where to start? *Pokémon Go* becomes boring very quickly (shock). *Endgame* is worth the wait; you'll work out what that is in due course. Your full head of hair will continue to recede whilst your metabolism begins to decline. When you read about *C***D-19* for the first time, you need to be ready. I mustn't continue, I've said far too much already.

So, what did we do? And yes, you are a miserable bastard, denial will only further your delusions of grandeur. We wrote a book, sort of. What we actually did was write a series of scripts for a television series that were compiled into a book. So, we somewhat wrote a book. This isn't remotely important.

I'll confess something amusing, you're going to enjoy telling people that you're writing a book before you've even put pen to paper. You'll think it makes you look interesting, sophisticated even. You'll even don a pair of clear glasses for a month in the summer of 2018 from a vintage boutique in Lincoln because somebody said you suited them. It even makes it into your *Tinder* bio for a couple of months. You might not be cringing now, but you will be. So hard.

There are a lot of things worth cringing over in the next six years. I suppose if we can't look back on our sad little life and wince every now and again then we're growing up wrong.

You know that playlist you're creating? That playlist with all the heart-breaking songs you listen to in the dark. You know the one, the playlist where you used an online thesaurus to find synonyms for the word 'sad' and discovered the word 'melancholy'? Yeah? Abandon it. Melancholy Days is not for you.

With a title like 'Melancholy Days' I can see why you'd think you're remark-ably profound and that's OK, you're 20. This is a formative time for you. Pair that mentality and dressing in black and somebody might just see you as a little more than the mediocre student you truly are.

But please, Melancholy Days is not for you. This is your final warning but I hope you don't listen to me. This title is going to pave the path for the next six years for you. I'm talking a playlist that leads to a book, then to a script, then back to being a book again and even births an Anti-Melancholy Days. The jubilant adversary of the original doom-monger.

Look, another sneak peek at what's to come, I can't say too much. You'll climb a 'mountain' in Barcelona, you'll wake on the floor of a ferry cabin shirtless, and you'll truly appreciate the importance of what man's best friend means. You're going to have contrasting jobs in different professions but stick to your writing, you enjoy writing. Also, please exercise more, drinking long after the party's over is not your friend but training for a half-marathon is.

I'm proud of you. You've got a lot to be proud of and it can be hard to appreciate that when you're alone. We'll always struggle with accepting ourself, even now. We're a work in progress.

I thought that writing to you would make me feel more introspective about our journey. I thought I might reel off the usual spiel you find in these types of letters. You know the sort, 'be kinder to yourself', 'know your worth', that kind of thing. I mean please do all of that because I remember how low your self-esteem is and negativity is corrosive. The point I'm trying to make is that to finish this chapter I need you to make mistakes.

I need you to meet the challenging characters that will make you feel meaningless. I need you to fail in different career paths so you can pick yourself back up, dust yourself off, and move on to the next one. That's always the hardest part because you'll have to contend with your own self-worth.

When you write this book, I want you to remember this is fiction. I want you to remember being too poor to buy loved ones Christmas presents and writing them postcards with apologies instead. I want you to remember finding a home in somebody important to you and welcoming their dog (your new best friend), even though you are a cat person.

Remember those drunk conversations with yourself in the mirrors of ugly pub toilets. Remember black eyes, feeling numb, addiction and desperation. Never forget the winter chill of an upstairs flat with no central heating on Boxing Day. Remember you are good enough to do this and you will succeed. Be proud of yourself now and you might change our prospective.

You're not always going to be this abstract in the future, but you'll understand what I'm talking about when the time comes. That chip on your shoulder, you need to lose it pal. Enjoy where you are now because things will become harder. You will make mistakes and life will become tough but that's OK.

Regression to the mean. Life's not always going to be good, but it's not always going to be bad either. Life always finds its way back to the middle.

All the best mate, well done,

You

MELANCHOLY DAYS

Pilot

ACT ONE

OVER BLACK.

SFX: *Muffled rush hour traffic and faint inaudible discussions between commuters fade in gradually.*

SFX: *Phone ringing.*

INT. BEDROOM   MORNING

MARC, late twenties, hungover and short tempered with most, he's trim but forgetfully average looking. Haunted by his past and drinking his demons, he believes himself to be one of the good guys. His eyes are tired and his facial hair is short and unkempt. He stands unblinking before his reflection wearing only his underwear as his phone continues to ring.

On the last dial of the phone call, he snaps out of his trance and looks down towards his phone resting on his unmade bed. Marc has missed the call.

>   MARC
>   Fuck. Shit.

He reaches down to pick his phone up and reads through his notifications.

>   PHONE NOTIFICATION
>   Two missed calls from Heather.

>   HEATHER (TEXT MESSAGE)
>   You need to stop calling me when
>   you're drunk, Marc. This has to
>   stop.

Marc throws his phone back onto the bed and turns back to face the mirror again. He examines his body before locking eye contact with himself. He sighs deeply.

>   MARC
>   Why are you like this?

TITLES OVER BLACK: MELANCHOLY DAYS

SFX: Glass breaking and shattering.

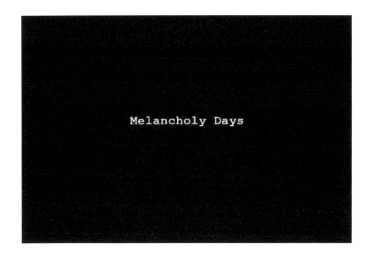

INT. BEDROOM   MOMENTS LATER

Now dressed in shirt and trousers, Marc stands looking out of the bay windows in his bedroom. He haphazardly adjusts his tie. He turns and reaches for his wristwatch on his bedside table.

Marc checks the time and realises he is late for work. He quickly exits his bedroom.

> MARC'S THOUGHTS
> (Rushed)
> Fuck, not again.

INT. KITCHEN   MOMENTS LATER

Sat on the kitchen countertop, SPENCE's head reclines in from the kitchen window as a cloud of cigarette smoke follows.

Spence, late twenties, he's gentle but lazy and unapologetically casual in both appearance and demeanour. Content in his own company and 'in between places', he's currently in his second year of living in a sleeping bag on the floor of Marc's unfurnished spare room.

Marc looks through the kitchen cupboards for some breakfast.

                    SPENCE

You shouldn't do that to yourself.

                    MARC'S THOUGHTS

Spence. Lives exclusively in a
sleeping bag on the floor of my
spare room. Unshakably lazy and in
between jobs... my other half.

                    MARC

Do what?

                    MARC'S THOUGHTS

I know exactly what he's talking
about.

Spence turns towards Marc from the window.

                    SPENCE

That thing you do in the mirror. You
know what I'm talking about. Staring
at yourself like that, you do it
every morning. It's self deprecat
ing and it makes you late for work.

Marc rolls his eyes.

                    MARC

And you should have left two years
ago but you haven't, you're still
here... sleeping on the floor. Are
you still looking for work?

                    SPENCE

I've got a few things in the
pipeline, banked up a lot of karma
recently. Something good's coming my
way.

                    MARC

Yeah, like it did when we left uni?

                    MARC'S THOUGHTS

Too far.

Marc acknowledges his comment as an awkward silence sits be

tween them.

> MARC
>
> I'll see you after group tonight.

> SPENCE
> (Hurt)
> Yeah, sure thing.

He turns and walks back towards his bedroom from the kitchen.

> SPENCE (O.S.)
> Oh, we need some milk and coffee by the way. We're nearly out.

To avoid snapping at him, Marc remains facing away from Spence.

> MARC
> **I'm** nearly out of milk and coffee, **I am** nearly out.

> SPENCE
> Yeah, you know, you, me, us. The same thing.

> MARC'S THOUGHTS
> It's really fucking not the same thing.

> MARC
> (Annoyed)
> Sure, whatever. I'll pick some up today. Got to go or I'll miss the tube, see you tonight.

INT. BEDROOM   MOMENTS LATER

Almost ready to leave for work, Marc reaches for his work bag and places it on his bedside table. He rummages through the bag.

> MARC'S THOUGHTS
> Keys, cigs, phone, crippling guilt, lingering anxiety... all here.

He stands up quickly and throws his bag over his shoulder. The bag knocks over a half empty bottle of whiskey and startles him slightly. He eyes a browning banana on his bedside table and hesitates to reach for it.

> MARC'S THOUGHTS
>
> Do I? Won't have time to go to the shop. Fuck it, pass. I'll see an other day if I don't.

He leaves the browning banana and exits.

INT. TUBE STATION   LATER THAT MORNING

The tube station is crowded. Marc stands eyeing his wristwatch. He glances down the platform and briefly locks eyes with a fellow commuter, she's beautiful.

> MARC'S THOUGHTS
>
> Fuck, I would literally eat glass for you.
>   (beat)
> No, don't be creepy.
>   (beat)
> Glass, definitely glass.

The tube arrives.

INT. TUBE CARRIAGE   MOMENTS LATER

The tube carriage is busy, commuters wrestle with each other to find standing space. As Marc squeezes into a small gap on the carriage, he grazes an older BUSINESSMAN with his workbag.

In his mid fifties, the Businessman is accomplished and very easily aggravated. Dressed in a grey suit and very fatigued looking, he's everything Marc wishes against becoming.

> MARC
>
> Sorry mate.

> BUSINESSMAN
>
> That's close enough.

> MARC
>   (Looking up, startled)
> I'm sorry, what?

> BUSINESSMAN

I said that's close enough 'mate'.
I'm not your fucking **mate**.

Both are pressed up against one another now, the tube is unwavering.

                    BUSINESSMAN
              (Under breath)
          I hate the tube.

                    MARC
              (Under breath)
          You and me both.

Marc doesn't know where to look. His eyes wander.

                    BUSINESSMAN
          Eyeing my watch, are you? Waiting
          for an opportunity to take it?

                    MARC
          No? Just going to work.

                    MARC'S THOUGHTS
          What the fuck is happening?

                    BUSINESSMAN
          You'll think twice next time you
          want to try it on with me son. I
          won't be taken for a **twat**, you hear
          me? I won't be taken for a **twat**.

                    MARC
          Look I'm sorry if I've upset you.
              (beat)
          I'm not quite sure what's happening
          here?

                    BUSINESSMAN
          Are you deaf boy? A **twat**, I won't be
          taken for one.

                    MARC'S THOUGHTS
          Say twat again.

The tube stops and a handful of commuters exit the carriage

freeing up space by a window for Marc to move into. Marc shuffles away from the Businessman and glances through the carriage window.

> MARC'S THOUGHTS
>> Should have told him where to go, could have even coughed on him. No, we're post pandemic now, I'm not an animal. I'll just give him a swift fucking off and run for the door.

Marc turns back towards the Businessman, he's psyched.

The Businessman has now proceeded to shuffle further down the carriage away from Marc and is out of earshot.

> MARC'S THOUGHTS
>> I don't know who was luckier here.

INT. TUBE STATION   MOMENTS LATER

The tube arrives at Marc's stop, he departs the carriage and looks back through the tube window. He catches the attention of the Businessman and they lock eyes. Marc smiles sarcastically and raises his middle finger to the Businessman through the carriage window as the tube doors shut.

As Marc lowers his middle finger he is passed by the beautiful commuter on the platform. She isn't afraid to hide her disgust for Marc's gesture. He cringes and lowers his arm by his side.

> CARA
>> What are you doing?

Marc is startled, he doesn't see CARA coming and is taken aback.

This is Cara, mid twenties, she's Irish and a close friend to Marc. She's dry and everybody's acquaintance but nobody's best friend. Her hard work complements her punctuality even if it comes at a personal cost. She's holding two takeaway coffees.

> MARC'S THOUGHTS
>> Cara, work, irritatingly punctual. We kissed at a work barbecue two years ago over a mini fridge and haven't spoken about it since.

                    MARC
               (Shocked)
          Shit! Cara, really?

Cara notices the beautiful commuter passing and glances acri
moniously towards Marc.

                    CARA
          You've got no chance, you know that
          right?

                    MARC
          I think the gesture did enough of
          the talking to secure that.

They begin walking for the exit of the tube.

                    CARA
          Gestures aside, do you really think
          she'd be into somebody as cynical or
          as narcissistic as you are?

                    MARC'S THOUGHTS
          I'm definitely both.

                    MARC
          I'm not cynical, I'm a realist,
          there's a difference. It's good to
          have an interest in yourself. It's
          healthy, a healthy obsession.

                    CARA
          Look, it wouldn't kill you to be a
          bit more positive about everything.
          You do tend to be bitter about
          things... you need to be better, not
          bitter. It's something the rest of
          us all seem to manage and if you
          don't agree then you've proved my
          point.

Both exit the tube station.

EXT. THE CITY   CONTINUOUS

They walk out of the tube station and into the city, Cara hands

Marc his takeaway coffee.

> CARA
>
> Anyway, here's your caffeine.

> MARC
> (Cringing)
> Don't call it caffeine. It's coffee.

> CARA
>
> It's the same fucking thing. You're welcome by the way.

> MARC
>
> What? For the coffee? Where did you get it from? The new place near *Prezzo?* I fucking love Italian.

Marc examines the cup.

> CARA
>
> No, not the coffee. The Ordinance report. Took half my Saturday to finish but it's done. Sara might ease off you a bit today.

> MARC'S THOUGHTS
>
> Shit.

Marc sips from his cup. He burns his tongue on the coffee.

> MARC
>
> Fuck, that's hot.
> (beat)
> Thanks, you shouldn't have come in on a Saturday to finish it. I was going to get the report finished eventually... I owe you a drink.

She brushes him off.

> CARA
>
> It's fine, the team needed it finishing last week. Let's get that drink soon and we'll call it even, yeah?

EXT. OFFICE BUILDING   CONTINUOUS

They arrive outside of the office building and stop to watch a STREET PERFORMER entertaining a small group of people. The Street Performer kneels on his right knee with both arms out stretched parallel to one another in front of him. He's wearing a scruffy high visibility jacket. He kneels silently, this is his act.

>   MARC
>
> This guy.
>   (beat)
> He's here every single day, doesn't
> speak, dance, sing, not even a dog.
> Everyday he's here and you know
> what? He probably makes more than we
> do.
>
>   CARA
>
> More than you do, don't include me
> in your pity party... how much are
> they paying you?
>   (beat)
> I bet he's wise.
>
>   MARC
>
> Clearly not wise enough, you can
> smell what I'm smelling right? His
> act is glorified pavement yoga and
> I'm certain I saw him drink from
> the fountain by the big *Pret* last
> weekend.

They both enter the office building.

INT. OFFICE FOYER   CONTINUOUS

They approach the foyer lift; Cara presses the button.

>   CARA
>
> How was your weekend anyway?
>
>   MARC
>
> A bit of self loathing and crying
> into the mirror, toilet *Netflix*.

Went the big *Tesco*. I mean if that
sounds good then yeah, a great week
end, I guess?
>   (beat)
> I did go a little far on Friday
> night though after work.

                    MARC'S THOUGHTS
That's a fucking understatement,
please don't mention the texts.

                    CARA
Yeah, I got your texts.

                    MARC'S THOUGHTS
Guilty.

                    MARC
Sorry about that.

SFX: Elevator doors opening.

The elevator doors open, both enter and turn towards the door
as it closes.

SFX: Elevator doors closing.

INT. ELEVATOR   CONTINUOUS

                    CARA
>   (Feigning positivity)
> I get it though, don't worry. Con
> nell ended things on Saturday...
> said I worked too much. Nothing *Uber
> Eats* and breakup wine can't fix.

                    MARC'S THOUGHTS
Shit, did I do that?

                    MARC
Sorry you had to cover, you
shouldn't have had to...

                    CARA
>   (Interrupting)
> Don't worry about it, I'll be fine.

> We'd been on and off for a while,
> he was really into *crypto* and feet
> stuff... a proper *Tarantino*. Nobody
> wants to go full *Tarantino*.

> MARC
>
> No, never full *Tarantino*.

> CARA
>
> He was beginning to give me the ick
> to be honest.

> MARC
>
> Shit. There's no coming back from
> that. We'll get that drink soon,
> promise.

> CARA
>
> This is fine, I'll be fine. We'll be
> fine.

> MARC'S THOUGHTS
>
> I think it's fine.

INT. MARC'S DESK   LATER THAT MORNING

Marc stares emptily at the dual screens of his desktop. His
gaze pans down towards a framed picture of himself and a girl,
he looks happy here. The frame is tucked behind a potted desk
plant, he reaches for it.

SFX: Pen hitting Marc's head.

Before he can look at the frame properly, Marc is struck in the
back of the head by a pen. He sits forward and turns to Cara.

> MARC
>
> What do you want?

> CARA
> (Whispering)
>
> Weekly team meeting, five minutes,
> come on Marc... I've emailed you
> about it twice.

He glances up at his desktop to see Cara's unread emails.

>   MARC
>   (Playing it cool)
>   Oh yeah, I know, got my list ready.
>   See you in there.

>   MARC'S THOUGHTS
>   I'm about as ready as an unwanted
>   pregnancy.

He looks down at his empty notepad. Marc has nothing.

INT. OFFICE MEETING ROOM   MOMENTS LATER

Marc takes a seat next to Cara; the large round table of the
meeting room starts to fill. One seat remains empty at the
front of the room.

>   CARA
>   Where is your list? Do you have
>   anything?

>   MARC
>   I'll be fine, trust me. I'll wing
>   it, always do. I think she's in a
>   good mood, we haven't heard any cry
>   ing yet.

>   CARA
>   Yeah, Steph hasn't had to run to the
>   bathroom in tears yet.
>   (beat)
>   She really hates you.

She finally enters the meeting room, her name is SARA. She's
in her mid thirties and uncommonly plain. She's tall and ill
tempered. Having been promoted to management early in her
career, she plays her cards close to her chest. The room sits
up straight, Marc remains slouched in his chair.

>   MARC'S THOUGHTS
>   Here we go, Hades with a handbag.

She stands over the empty chair and scans the room silently.

>   SARA
>   (Accusatory)

Cara, I know what you did.

> MARC'S THOUGHTS

Weird way to start a meeting.

> SARA

You covered for Marc this weekend, didn't you?
> (beat)
Your key card doesn't lie. Steph filled me in this morning.

Both Marc and Cara look towards STEPH in disbelief.

> CARA

I'm sorry, the client expected it on Friday. They've been chasing the re port for weeks.

> SARA

And why wasn't it finished on time, Marc?

All eyes are on Marc.

> MARC
> (Playing it cool)

Well, you remember when the server went down last week? That happened. The clocks also went forward. I had a lot of shredding to do, GDPR stuff really, you know how fast the time flies around here.

> MARC'S THOUGHTS

That last one's not even a lie. Can't they just pay me to shred things all the time?

> SARA

So, nothing of real substance then, Marc?
> (beat)
For **fuck's sake**, we have deadlines to meet for a reason. Not meeting them is unacceptable and yet again

you're weighing this team down with
your incompetence. If it continues
then the next step is disciplinary
action. Don't fuck this team over
again.
          (beat)
What do you have on this week?

                    MARC
I'm in between reports, need to call
Ransom back about their finance re
ports, monthly KPI's, plenty to keep
me busy.

Sara, unmoved.

                    SARA
It's this blasé attitude to your
work that slows the rest of this
team down, Marc. By the sounds of
it, you have some capacity if not
flexibility then?

                    MARC'S THOUGHTS
What the fuck does that even mean?
Where has she pulled that from?

                    MARC
          (Apprehensively)
Yeah, I guess?

                    SARA
Excellent, you can take on the
yearly performance report for the
shareholders then. I want it format
ted and emailed to me by the end of
the day tomorrow.

                    MARC
You'll have it by lunch.

                    SARA
No, I want it at the end of the day.
          (beat)
Oh, and Cara, grow a backbone. He
wouldn't come in on a Saturday for

you. Don't let his ineptitude bring
your performance down. You're better
than that.

                    CARA
Yes, definitely. Thank you, Sara.

                    MARC'S THOUGHTS
Kill me.

INT. OFFICE MEETING ROOM   AFTER THE MEETING

The meeting has just finished, Marc remains in his seat.
Defeated, he once again glances down at his empty notepad on
the table. He sighs and slowly rests his head on the table be
fore him.

END OF ACT ONE

ACT TWO

INT. OFFICE CAFETERIA   LUNCHTIME

Cara is sat alone at a free table, her lunch is a poorly constructed Mediterranean Mezze Platter, it fills the table. Marc sits down abruptly, he's frustrated. He fixates on Steph sitting on a nearby table, she's reading through important work documents.

> MARC
>
> Look at her, over there.

> CARA
> (Confused)
>
> Who?

> MARC
>
> Fucking Steph, the nerve of her, honestly.

He gestures towards her.

> CARA
>
> I'm confused, what's happened now?

> MARC
>
> You know she's microwaved salmon again... she did it twice last week. Gassing out the office. Nobody should eat that much salmon.
> (beat)
> I don't know. I thought she was one of us.

> CARA
>
> So, it's her dinner that's pissed you off? Not the report?

> MARC
>
> You know she shits in the disabled

toilet, right?

> CARA
> (Defeated)
> Just let it go, Marc. Sara was always going to find out about the report, you don't write them as well as I do.

Marc brings his attention back to the table. He examines Cara's lunch.

> MARC
> What is all of this?

> CARA
> I did a big shop before Connell left and didn't have the heart to let it all go to waste.
> (beat)
> I mean I've never really shied away from eating my feelings after a break up in the past so why stop now? What do you have?

She looks around for his lunch.

> MARC
> Just caffeine for me.

> MARC'S THOUGHTS
> I hate myself for that.

> CARA
> (Smugly)
> **Ha!** Told you it would catch on.

> MARC
> Barely, I need a smoke. See you soon.

Marc stands and walks towards the cafeteria exit; he walks by Steph's table. With one hand he reaches for his cigarettes whilst the other purposefully knocks Steph's documents onto the floor.

Whilst he instantly regrets his actions, he's too proud to turn around and pick them back up in front of the cafeteria. Marc exits.

INT. MARC'S DESK   AFTERNOON

Back at his desk, Marc struggles to get started with work.

SFX: Email notification.

Marc is startled. He opens the email, it's a GIF of an overweight cat from Cara. He struggles to feign a genuine smile back towards her desk.

SFX: Text message notification.

Marc, startled again, reaches for his phone from his trouser pocket and reads the text.

> LIV (TEXT MESSAGE)
> *MARC! I need to see you now, it's an emergency, meet me at Cross Keys in town ASAP?xx*

> MARC'S THOUGHTS
> Now? Really? I hate that place, must be important. She only really texts for sex. A sex emergency maybe?
> (beat)
> What the fuck am I talking about?

He glances up anxiously towards Sara's office, he's trying to determine whether she's in a good mood.

INT. SARA'S OFFICE   MOMENTS LATER

Marc stands before Sara, he's nervous and can't stop rubbing the back of his head.

> MARC
> I wouldn't ask unless it was an emergency, I really wouldn't, but you see my boiler's been on its way out and it's finally packed in. My flatmate's just been on the phone, loads of tears, water everywhere, big problem. I need to call the men

in.

>   SARA
>   (Unconvinced)
> The men?

>   MARC
> You know, the real men. The type who
> deals with this kind of thing, tool
> box owners, not me, never me.
>   (beat)
> I got a splinter from a handrail
> this morning, I'm not equipped to be
> dealing with this kind of thing. The
> manly stuff.

>   MARC'S THOUGHTS
> Is this... working?

>   SARA
> Why can't your flatmate call them?

>   MARC
>   (Countering)
> He doesn't have the numbers, I'd
> rather call them myself, he's new, a
> new flatmate. Only just moved in.

>   MARC'S THOUGHTS
> Two years on the floor, two years in
> the way, does that still count as
> new?

Sara glares up slowly from her screen.

>   SARA
> I'm not sure I made myself quite
> clear this morning, you're on very
> thin ice, Marc. I'm not happy about
> this and quite frankly I don't be
> lieve you. I think you're bullshit
> ting me.
>   (beat)
> We're keeping a very close eye on
> you at the moment. Your appraisal is

next month and I'll be honest with
you, it's not looking good.
>   (beat)
However, that said, I know how dif
ficult it can be.

>   MARC

Exactly, we all need hot water.

>   SARA

No, having flatmates.

>   MARC'S THOUGHTS

Not going to poke that bear.

>   MARC

So, am I OK to?

He gestures towards the office door.

>   SARA
>   (Seriously)
You can go... **but,** if we, no, if
I find out this is anything other
than your boiler then I will be ter
minating your employment with this
agency. Have I made myself clear,
Marc?

>   MARC

Absolutely. Crystal.

>   SARA

I still want the shareholder's re
port on my desk by the end of tomor
row. No exceptions.

>   MARC

Of course, you'll have it tomorrow.

He begins to shuffle away from her desk.

>   MARC'S THOUGHTS

Now to unclench my arsehole, unroll
my toes and back out of the room
slowly like I'm not dropping every

> thing for someone who refuses to leave a toothbrush at mine because it 'sends the wrong message'.

INT. CROSS KEYS   LATER THAT AFTERNOON

Marc enters the bar and scans the room. The bar is relatively empty, an elderly man sits in the corner reading a newspaper as the bartender stands scrolling through his phone. He walks to the bar.

> MARC
>
> Pint of *Neck Oil* please... pal.

> MARC'S THOUGHTS
>
> Pal?
> (beat)
> Is this wise?

Marc pays the bartender via contactless and sips from his beverage. He waits by the bar.

SFX: Toilet door opening.

Marc turns to see her exiting the toilet, this is LIV. She's in her early twenties and younger than Marc. She's beautifully destructive as the rest of the world is merely a supporting character in her own selfish story. Accustomed to getting her own way, life always falls just right for her no matter the damage it causes others. They're fucking.

She approaches Marc at the bar.

> MARC'S THOUGHTS
>
> Liv, I usually see her after dark, she's usually shit faced. Rude to me ninety percent of the time, passed out in my bed the remaining ten.

> MARC
>
> How long have you been in there?

> LIV
> (Annoyed)
> Why do you have a drink?

Marc is confused.

                    MARC

We're in a bar?

                    LIV

What do you think this is? It's a
Monday afternoon Marc?

                    MARC

You said you needed to see me. **In a
bar**. Are we not meeting for a drink?

                    LIV

Jesus Christ, I text you saying it
was an emergency and your first in
stinct is to buy a drink. Fight or
flight and you're reaching for the
nearest bottle, fucking hell Marc.
        (beat)
No, I just needed a piss, and this
was the closest public toilet I
wasn't likely to contract syphilis
from. You know we're not together
Marc, we don't do that. We're just
fucking. **No strings**.

                    MARC

I'm sorry? You can see my confusion
though, right? I just thought it
might be a little courteous for one
of us to at least buy a drink given
that we are meeting **in a bar**.
        (beat)
And there's nothing more calming
than a Monday afternoon pint in an
empty bar. Doesn't scream quarter
life crisis, does it?

Liv rolls her eyes.

                    LIV

We agreed you wouldn't do your self
loathe thing with me, just sex and
now emergencies apparently.

                MARC'S THOUGHTS

There are services for this kind of thing.

                    MARC
Yeah, sure. What's the emergency?

Liv glances toward the bartender anxiously, she's acting shifty. The bartender is still occupied scrolling through his phone.

                    LIV
               (Whispering)
I need you to carry some coke and a couple of pills for me. I have an interview this afternoon and appar ently the security on the door give you a thorough pat down and search your bags. I don't want to risk it. I told you about the interview, remember?

                    MARC'S THOUGHTS
No.

                    MARC
Oh yeah, shit. Is that today?

                    LIV
I need this job Marc, my student loan is fucking me, please? It's just a one time thing.

He's thinking about it.

                    LIV
               (Desperately)
I'll... I'll stay tonight when I pick them up? Carry on where we left off on Friday? Please, Marc? I need this.

He's anxious about helping her.

                    MARC'S THOUGHTS
I'm absolutely going to do this, aren't I?

                    MARC
          Fuck, yes OK. Pick them up tonight.
          This is a favour, a one time thing,
          just for today.

                    LIV
          Of course, yeah, promise.

She hands the bag to him discreetly; he slides it into the back
pocket of his trousers. She looks towards the exit.

                    LIV
                 (Relieved)
          Look, I have to go now. Enjoy your
          sad Monday drink, you look rough
          today, real homeless vibes. Just an
          FYI.

                    MARC'S THOUGHTS
          Pretend you didn't hear that.

                    MARC
          Good one. Good luck with the inter
          view.
               (beat)
          You bitch.

                    LIV
          What?

                    MARC
          Erm, nothing. It was nothing.

She stands and exits the bar. Marc looks down at his now empty
pint glass and sighs regretfully. He catches the attention of
the bartender.

                    MARC
          Same again please mate... and I'll
          take a whiskey too, house, make it a
          double please?

The bartender begins pouring his second pint. As Marc waits, he
re reads his text message from Heather that morning. He glances
up regretfully before downing his double whiskey and sighing in

a dramatic fashion.

END OF ACT TWO

ACT THREE

EXT. THE COMMUNITY CENTRE   EVENING

Hours have passed since the bar. A tipsy Marc stands outside of an inner city community centre. Marc attends a weekly mental health support group, it settles him. He stands outside the entrance smoking a cigarette, he's tipsier than he initially anticipated after leaving the bar.

Fellow group members begin to arrive and enter the community centre, Marc chooses to be distant from them.

> MARC
>
> Yeah, hey.
> > (beat)
> Hi.

INT. THE COMMUNITY CENTRE   LATER

Marc enters and struggles to take his jacket off; he hangs it on a coat stand and searches for an available seat in the room. The chairs in the room are arranged in a circle for roughly 15 people. Marc sits and the group begins shortly after.

A lady stands from the circle, this is the GROUP LEADER, she's in her mid sixties. She's slender with wiry grey hair but a kind soul at heart.

> MARC'S THOUGHTS
>
> The Group Leader, never did catch
> her name, too late to ask now.

> GROUP LEADER
> > (To the group)
> Good evening to those I haven't
> already spoken to yet. I'd like to
> thank you all for being here with us
> tonight.
> > (beat)
> To those coming back each week I'd
> like to thank you for being brave

and continuing your journey and keeping my lights on. It's great to see some new faces here tonight as well...

The room claps awkwardly.

> GROUP LEADER
>
> It's hard enough admitting we have a problem. Taking those next steps to seek help is even harder. I'm proud of all of you for making it here tonight. Coming to terms with our feelings and mental well being can be tough and that's why we keep com ing back to these sessions to help and support each other through the darkness.
> (beat)
> There are no right or wrong answers in these sessions, we're here to listen and hopefully... heal our minds in the process.

> MARC'S THOUGHTS
>
> Heal our minds? They used to fucking lobotomise people like us.

The Group Leader turns to NEIL. He's a wheelchair user in his mid forties. He's sat opposite Marc.

> GROUP LEADER
>
> Neil, do you want to start us off this week? How have you been? Any news?

> MARC'S THOUGHTS
>
> Need a piss. Dark trousers, could I get away with a little wee on the chair? No, it's an unstoppable hose once the floodgates open.

> NEIL
>
> Not a terrible week. Feeling a bit of angst from ma's new guide dog, he's threatened by my chair.

>   (beat)
> Did win on a scratch card this morn
> ing. Not enough for the leg surgery
> or a plane ticket to Switzerland but
> you know, silver linings.

>   MARC'S THOUGHTS
> Fucking hell Neil.
>   (beat)
> I wish they'd euthanise me... or
> section me, I'm not picky.

>   GROUP LEADER
> Erm, thank you for that, Neil.

The focus in the room moves from Neil to Marc.

>   GROUP LEADER
> And what about you Marc? Are you
> finally ready to open up to us this
> week?

>   MARC'S THOUGHTS
> Cards to your chest, poker face. No,
> you're feeling better today.

Marc sits awkwardly, he can feel the room watching him. His
chest begins to tighten as he reaches for his heart. He can
feel himself sobering up, this is an uncomfortable experience.

>   MARC
> I don't think... I'm not there yet.
> Well, I mean I am... I'm just a
> bit stuck and... so is she, more so
> than I am... the guilt is so fucking
> heavy.

He glances painfully at Neil's wheelchair.

>   MARC
>   (Deflecting)
> Erm, you know I'm half cut right
> now. I left work early because I
> thought somebody needed me because I
> thought I could help but...
>   (beat)

> No, forget it, not tonight. I'm
> sorry I can't do this. I'm not
> ready yet. I need another week. But
> hey, at least I'll be able to sleep
> tonight.

He gestures a drinking motion with his right hand.

                    GROUP LEADER
> And why did you drink today? Why
> didn't you stay at work?

                    MARC
                 (Uncomfortably)
> I didn't realise she only needed a
> piss.

                    GROUP LEADER
> What?

                    MARC
> It doesn't matter. I'm here, aren't
> I? It's enough... enough for me.

                    GROUP LEADER
> That's true Marc but we can't heal
> ourselves until with help ourselves.

                    MARC'S THOUGHTS
> She definitely has that crocheted on
> a cushion.

Marc sits silently, reflecting on his outburst.

                    GROUP LEADER
> OK Marc, next week perhaps.

She turns from Marc; the spotlight has finally shifted.

                    GROUP LEADER (O.S.)
> What about you Mary? You must be
> coming up to your third month clean?
> How is everything?

MARY, in her forties and very bedraggled. She is a recovering
heroin addict with rumpled hair and an uncomfortable twitch.

The group discussion fades out as the camera fixes on Marc. He's zoned out of the session, his mind wanders. The world con tinues around him.

INT. THE COMMUNITY CENTRE   LATER

The group has finished and members are leaving the building. Marc struggles to put his jacket on, he's still tipsy. Marc is approached by the Group Leader.

> GROUP LEADER
>
> It's coming Marc, you'll be able to talk about it soon. Just make sure you keep coming to group, it'll get easier. I've been where you are, just make sure you come back next week.

> MARC
>
> Thanks, I will.

> GROUP LEADER
>
> You have to.

> MARC'S THOUGHTS
>
> Was that a threat?

> MARC
>
> Yeah, I know. I never miss a session.

> GROUP LEADER
>
> No, you have to. It's your turn to bring the biscuits. We have a system so we kinda' have to see you next week. Don't bake, just buy them, no body likes a try hard here.
> (beat)
> And be sober next week, please? Reflects poorly on me letting in drunks to a support group.

After struggling with his zip, Marc contorts his body and manages to finally zip his jacket up towards his neck. In doing so he unknowingly drops Liv's bag from his trouser pocket. He turns to the Group Leader.

>   MARC
>   Uh, sure, got you. See you then.

Before he has a chance to notice the bag has fallen from his pocket, Mary reaches down and snatches Liv's drugs and exits the community centre swiftly.

>   GROUP LEADER
>   There's a sadness about you Marc,
>   it's OK to feel the way that you do.
>   We're here to help.

>   MARC
>   Yeah, that's why I keep coming back.
>   (beat)
>   Bye... then.

>   GROUP LEADER
>   Oh... bye then.

He nods to the Group Leader and exits awkwardly; this suddenly feels all too real for him.

INT. TUBE CARRIAGE   NIGHT

Marc stands with his head pressed up against the glass of the tube window listening to his *AirPods*. The tube carriage is quiet. Marc catches his reflection and glares briefly at himself before noticing the Businessman from earlier that morn ing further down the carriage.

The Businessman sits slumped against a different passenger asleep. In one hand he carries an empty bottle of cheap vodka, the other rests on a box of his belongings. It's clear that the Businessman lost his job today.

Marc turns back towards the tube window and smiles back at his reflection.

>   MARC'S THOUGHTS
>   Twat.

INT. MARC'S FLAT HALLWAY   LATER

Marc shuts the door behind him to his flat. He turns and rests his back against the shut door and looks up to the ceiling. His eyes are closed, he's relieved to be home.

                     MARC'S THOUGHTS
      Better not bitter, better not bit
      ter.

Spence rears his head from the spare room.

                     SPENCE
      So... did you get the milk? Coffee?

                     MARC
      What? Oh, no. Sorry, weird day. I'll
      pick some up tomorrow.

                     SPENCE
          (Disappointedly)
      Come on, really?

Marc snaps.

                     MARC
      Yes, **really**. Are you kidding me?
          (beat)
      You know you can leave whenever you
      want to get some yourself? I cut
      you a key to the flat for this very
      reason, so you can leave whenever
      you please. Fuck, why not get cof
      fee delivered here instead? You know
      they drone things out now? Hell, why
      don't you drone yourself out of my
      spare room and somewhere else?

Both stand puzzled.

                     MARC'S THOUGHTS
      I think you've lost us both there.

                     SPENCE
      Sorry, I didn't mean... Have you
      been drinking?

Marc deflects.

                     MARC

> I'm sorry man, weird day. Neil at group had something about a blind dog in Switzerland or something. I'll get them tomorrow, promise. I think I've got a hotel cappuccino sachet I was saving for my birthday somewhere, I'll get it for you.

> SPENCE
> No, don't worry about it, I'm sorry I asked. I'll be out of here soon, I just need a bit more time. Night.

Spence closes the spare room door on Marc for the night.

> MARC
> Night, mate.

INT. BEDROOM   MOMENTS LATER

Marc slumps onto his bed, he turns on his bedside table lamp. He pours himself a neat whiskey from the bottle by the side of his bed, his cup is dirty from the night before. He sighs and looks at his wristwatch before sitting further back onto his bed.

> MARC'S THOUGHTS
> Sleep now, that's eight hours until I have to be up for work. No hang over, one more drink to send me on my way.

Marc reaches for his glass before being interrupted.

SFX: Phone ringing.

Liv is calling.

> MARC'S THOUGHTS
> Shit.

Marc answers the phone to a drunk Liv.

> MARC
> (Into phone)
> Hi, you alright?

> LIV (V.O.)
> (Slurring)

I didn't, I didn't get the job, d
do you have my gear? I need it. I'm
outside, l let me in.

Marc stands and looks out from the bay windows of his bedroom.
Liv is sitting on the floor outside of his building, she waves
up to his window.

> MARC
> (Into phone)

Why are you on the floor?

> LIV (V.O.)
> (Slurring)

I, I, just needed to calm my nerves.
I'm not as bad as you were on F
Friday.

> MARC'S THOUGHTS

Definitely worse. Need to find out
what happened on Friday.

> LIV (V.O.)
> (Slurring)

Are you going to let me in or do I
have to call S Spence?

> MARC
> (Into phone)

Fine, but water when you get in.
Don't be sick like you were last
time.

> LIV (V.O.)
> (Slurring)

Promises, promises.

INT. BEDROOM   MOMENTS LATER

Liv sits on Marc's bed swaying; her make up is smudged. She
is not OK. Marc enters with a glass of water and two slices
of bread; she ignores him and reaches for his glass of whis
key instead.

                    MARC
No, no, no. Water and bread, please.

                    LIV
               (Slurring)
Do you have my b bag?

He doesn't want to give it to her but reluctantly reaches for the bag in the back pocket of his trousers. He can't find the bag. He frantically reaches into all of his pockets for a fur ther inspection.

                    MARC
               (Panicking)
Shit, I don't have it. It's got to be in here somewhere.

                    LIV
               (Slurring, angrily)
Marc, where the fuck is it? You've taken it all, haven't you? I knew this would happen.

                    MARC
No, I wouldn't, you know I'm clean.

                    LIV
               (Slurring)
I can't trust you, Marc. Nobody can. She trusted you and look where she ended up, you fuck everything up.

                    MARC
               (Angrily)
Excuse me?

                    LIV
               (Slurring)
Yeah, I know about her. You talk about her in your sleep. I c can't trust you.

                    MARC
You can, you can trust me, I don't...

> LIV
> (Interrupting, slurring)
>
> You're going to pay me back Marc,
> I'm serious. I'm going to sleep here
> tonight, you owe me that much. I'd
> *Uber* home but they've b blocked my
> account so I'm going to pass out
> here.
> (beat)
> Don't, don't touch me. You've really
> **fucked** me off.

Marc downs his whiskey and places the glass on his bedside table, he's disappointed in himself. He lays back on his bed and looks up at his ceiling, Liv passes out onto his chest.

The camera hangs over Marc's face and zooms in slowly. The light in the room dims as Marc embraces the darkness. As the camera zooms towards the centre of his face, he brings his phone to his ear.

SFX: Phone dialling out.

Heather answers.

> MARC
> (Into phone)
>
> Heather?

> HEATHER (V.O.)
>
> I told you to stop calling me, Marc.
> Goodnight.

She hangs up before Marc has an opportunity to reply.

SFX: Dead phone line.

CUT TO BLACK.

END OF PILOT

MELANCHOLY DAYS

Episode Two

ACT ONE

OVER BLACK.

SFX: A busy tube station. Faint inaudible discussions between commuters fade in gradually.

> TANNOY OPERATIVE (V.O.)
> We apologise for the delay to this
> morning's service. Thank you for
> your patience.

INT. TUBE PLATFORM   EARLY MORNING

MARC stands leant against the platform wall of the tube station. He's looking downward to the platform as his right hand clasps his face, he's hungover. With the same hand, he the clutches the bridge of his nose as his eyes close. He's late for work, again.

With anxiety setting in, he thrusts from the wall to glance down the platform for the tube, his restlessness is evident. Two ELDERLY PASSENGERS stagger beside him on the platform. He checks his wristwatch.

> MARC
> (Under breath)
> Come on. Not today, where the fuck
> is the tube?

The tube slowly emerges from the tunnel.

> MARC
> (Relieved, loudly)
> Oh my fucking god! Thank you.

The Elderly Passengers are taken aback. They share a similar expression of horror as the tube grinds to a gradual halt.

SFX: Carriage doors opening.

Marc angles to the Elderly Passengers apologetically.

> MARC
>
> Sorry, sorry about that.

TITLES OVER BLACK: MELANCHOLY DAYS

SFX: Glass breaking and shattering.

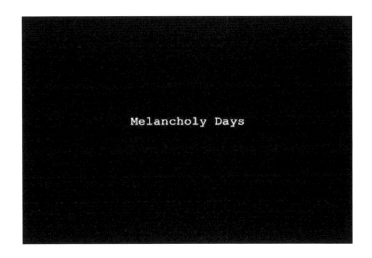

EXT. THE TUBE STATION EXIT   LATER

Marc exits the tube station and sprints into the city.

EXT. THE CITY   CONTINUOUS

Sprinting through the morning crowds, Marc jostles past bystanders whilst signalling apologetically to those he rico chets into before continuing his journey.

EXT. A CITY LAMPPOST   CONTINUOUS

Marc stops at a lamppost to catch his breath. He scrambles for his phone from his trouser pocket and reads his messages.

> CARA (TEXT MESSAGE)
>
> *Are you coming in today?*

> CARA (TEXT MESSAGE)
>
> *???*

>   CARA (TEXT MESSAGE)
>   *Where are you? She's already here!!*

Marc holsters his phone into his trouser pocket and sighs frustratingly before continuing his sprint through the city.

>   MARC'S THOUGHTS
>   (Short of breath)
>   So unfit. So unwell. So much misery.

EXT. THE CITY   CONTINUOUS

He sprints through the city and passes the STREET PERFORMER from the Pilot, he's close to the office.

INT. OFFICE FOYER   MOMENTS LATER

Marc speed walks into the officer foyer and stands before the elevator. He presses the button immediately before bending forward to catch his breath again. His heavy breathing turns into wheezing as he attempts to compose himself. He wipes the sweat from his forehead.

As he waits for the elevator, Marc is unknowingly joined by the company's MANAGING DIRECTOR. In his late fifties, the Managing Director is dressed head to toe in an expensive black suit with polished brogues to match. This man is the epitome of distinguished. Marc, still bent forward, can only see him from the waist down in his fragile state.

>   MANAGING DIRECTOR
>   (Sympathetically)
>   Are you alright there?

Marc remains hunched forward, he's still catching his breath.

>   MARC
>   (Short of breath)
>   Yeah... no... not really. Late for
>   work, the tube fucked me, hungover,
>   can't catch a break.

>   MARC'S THOUGHTS
>   You can say that again.

>   MARC

>   (Desperately)
>   Can you smell me? Do I smell? I
>   smell, don't I? Just what I need.

>   MANAGING DIRECTOR
>   Late night, was it?

Marc stands upright slowly as the elevator arrives. He hasn't registered who he's talking to.

SFX: Elevator arriving.

>   MARC
>   Not really. Well, a few drinks after
>   work, you know   the usual. Pints,
>   venting, more pints. Then a pub
>   quiz, another bar after that.
>   (beat)
>   Then a kebab, got it everywhere
>   obviously. A few drinks at mine and
>   then one, no, two... yeah, it took
>   two nightcaps to put me down.

>   MARC'S THOUGHTS
>   Too much information?

SFX: Elevator doors opening.

The elevator doors open as both enter; Marc ignorantly enters before the Managing Director.

INT. ELEVATOR   CONTINUOUS

Both enter and turn to face the elevator doors.

>   MARC
>   OK yeah, you got me, it was a late
>   night. The tube being late was a
>   real fuck you to my morning as well.
>   What's all that about?

>   MARC'S THOUGHTS
>   Definitely still drunk.

>   MANAGING DIRECTOR
>   Was the tube late or were you late
>   getting on the tube?

Marc presses the elevator button for the third floor.

> MARC
>
> OK, yeah. Got me again smart arse, guilty, but the tube was also late... what floor you on?

The Managing Director appears amused by Marc's story.

> MANAGING DIRECTOR
>
> The same one.

> MARC
>
> Cool, cool.

SFX: Elevator rides upwards.

The elevator falls silent as they both ride to the office floor. There's now an atmosphere between them.

> MARC'S THOUGHTS
>
> Way too old to be an intern, he does look familiar. Smells how real men should smell, powerful.
> (beat)
> I hope he can't smell my breath.

The elevator sways slightly on the incline and shakes inter mittently. Not helping with his hangover, Marc vomits into his closed mouth before having to swallow it back down to not raise suspicion. His eyes begin to tear up.

The elevator arrives at the office floor and both exit.

SFX: Elevator door opening.

INT. THE OFFICE   CONTINUOUS

Marc enters the office first and stumbles towards his desk. The Managing Director follows him at a short distance.

> MANAGING DIRECTOR
> (Over the office)
>
> Oh... and Marc, can you join us in the meeting room in ten minutes? No need to bring anything, we'll let you catch your breath first of

course, I know it was a heavy night.

> MARC
> (Confused)

Yeah, sure.

> MARC'S THOUGHTS

Fuck.

The Managing Director turns from Marc and walks straight into SARA's office.

INT. MARC'S DESK   MOMENTS LATER

Marc slumps into his desk chair and holds his head tightly. He reaches for a stale glass of desk water and sips from it slowly. CARA rolls her chair over to his desk quietly. Her presence frightens him.

> MARC
> (Shocked)

Shit. Stop creeping up on me like that, I'm fragile.

> CARA
> (Angrily)

Where the fuck have you been?

> MARC

I slept in, the tube was late. I'm not going through the list again. Who is that? I recognise him.

> CARA
> (Disbelief)

Who is **that**? Do you really not know? You're shitting me right now?

> MARC'S THOUGHTS

No.

> MARC

Yeah, of course I know. I've just forgotten his name. Can you just?

> CARA

(Whispering)

Paul Harvey. It's Paul **fucking** Har
vey, Marc? Managing Director? You
met him at the barbecue when we, you
know?

                    MARC'S THOUGHTS

Kissed and never talked about it
again.

                    MARC

Oh. Yeah, I remember. He told me
they want to see me in the meeting
room in ten minutes.

                    CARA

Yeah, we all heard. That's not good,
really not good   he only really
comes into the office to fire people
or charge his phone. God.
        (beat)
You smell... revolting.

                    MARC
                    (Worryingly)

Fuck. I just told him about last
night. He knows everything.

Cara cringes.

                    CARA

I told you to leave with me after
the quiz, you never listen. You
don't know when to stop.

                    MARC

Cara, we have bigger problems to
deal with right now. My burgeoning
alcoholism being the least of our
worries. We need to focus on getting
me through this meeting first.

                    MARC'S THOUGHTS

Or maybe we could think bigger pic
ture like my depression, nicotine

> addiction, crippling debt, take your
> pick.

Both sit back and think.

>   CARA
> No, you're right.
>   (beat)
> Just... keep smiling, nodding and
> agreeing. By all means don't be
> yourself. Act like you want to be
> here.

>   MARC
> Sure, got it, act like I know what
> this company does. I can do that.
> It's just a meeting. It's probably
> nothing.

>   CARA
> Yeah, it's not like they're going to
> fire you.

INT. OFFICE MEETING ROOM   MOMENTS LATER

Hard cut to Marc sitting opposite Sara and the Managing Dir
ector in the meeting room.

>   MANAGING DIRECTOR
> We're firing you.

There's an awkward silence.

>   MARC
> What? Sorry, pardon?

>   SARA
> I'm afraid today will be your last
> day with us, Marc.

>   MARC
> Well, this... is a surprise.

>   MARC'S THOUGHTS
> Even you don't believe that.

Sara shakes her head in disbelief.

                    SARA
I don't really think that it is
Marc.
        (beat)
You're late for work more often than
you are on time. You're behind on
your reports and your blasé attitude
is a careless representation of your
work ethic.
        (beat)
And Steph's informed me you've been
stealing from the stationery cup
board? Have I missed anything here?

                MARC'S THOUGHTS
Don't mention the stolen toilet
rolls.

                    MARC
No, don't think so.

The Managing Director readies himself for exposition.

                MANAGING DIRECTOR
Marc, the success of this business
is extremely important to us. I'm
sure you can understand and appreci
ate that.
        (beat)
The people we employ here need
to reflect that same attitude. For
quite some time now we've felt as
though you haven't been as on brand
with the company as we'd expect from
one of our employees.
        (beat)
We gave you the benefit of the
doubt given your... troubled past.
We thought you might have needed
some time to settle into the role
but time and again you've proven us
wrong and let the company down.
        (beat)
We simply can't tolerate behaviour

like yours Marc and I'm afraid we
are going to have to let you go
today.

> SARA
> (Interrupting)

Thank you, Paul, well said. We just
can't tolerate behaviour like yours
Marc, we're going to have to let you
go.

> MARC'S THOUGHTS

She's just fucking copied him.

> MARC

Do you want me to collect my things
and go now?

> MANAGING DIRECTOR

We think that would be wise.

Sara sits forward, holier than thou.

> SARA

Yeah. We think that would be wise.

Marc rises from his chair slowly.

> SARA

It feels like we're in a way putting
you out of your misery here Marc,
this is for your own good.

> MARC'S THOUGHTS

Like *Ted Bundy* on the electric
chair, he loved what he did.

> MARC

OK?

> MANAGING DIRECTOR

Is there anything else you'd like to
add before you go?

> MARC

No.

>   (beat)
>   I mean, I'm not going to give you
>   the satisfaction of telling you I
>   enjoyed my time here or thank you
>   for the experiences I've had because
>   I'd be lying... and I'm trying to be
>   more **on brand.**

>   MARC'S THOUGHTS
>   Ease back you still need the refer
>   ence.

He turns to the door before glancing back.

>   MARC
>   But, for what it's worth, I do
>   appreciate the honesty. Thank you
>   for the stationery... and the toilet
>   rolls.

>   MARC'S THOUGHTS
>   Can't fire me twice.

Marc nods toward the Managing Director and ignores Sara. He leaves the meeting room politely.

INT. THE OFFICE   CONTINUOUS

SFX: Door closing.

Marc shuts the door to the meeting room and faces the office, all eyes are on him. He's frozen.

>   MARC'S THOUGHTS
>   Be the bigger man, leave slowly with
>   your dignity relatively intact. Do
>   not by any means cause a scene. Bet
>   ter not bitter, better not bitter...

He storms back into the meeting room.

INT. OFFICE MEETING ROOM   CONTINUOUS

The door flies open and Marc re enters as the Managing Director and Sara are sat talking amongst themselves. He thrusts a pointed finger towards Sara.

> MARC
> (Shouting)

You know I was the only person who thanked you for that foul cake you baked for Steph's birthday. It was truly revolting, like eating a mis erable sandbag but I thanked you for it because it was kind. A kind thing to do for someone. I appreciated the effort **you** made for her because somebody needed to.

He begins pointing towards the office floor with his opposite hand.

> MARC
> (Still shouting)

You know they hate you out there, they all do. I hear it every day. Not a single one of them has a good word to say about you when your back's turned.

> MANAGING DIRECTOR

You should go before you say some thing you'll regret Marc.

> MARC

Oh fuck off Paul.

Marc realises the severity of his outburst. He turns abruptly and leaves the meeting room.

SFX: Door slamming.

INT. MARC'S DESK   MOMENTS LATER

Marc slumps into his desk chair and slowly lowers his forehead onto the desk before groaning. All eyes are still on him.

> MARC
> (Under breath)

Fuck, fuck, fuck.

Cara wheels her chair over to his desk quickly.

                    CARA
                (Concerned)
        What just happened? Why were you
        shouting about sandbags?

                    MARC
        They fired me. You were right.
        Should have seen it coming.

                    CARA
        What? No. I didn't think they actu
        ally would. They can't just? You're
        fucking with me, right?

Marc raises his head to eye level with Cara and begins to pack
up his belongings.

                    MARC
        Nah, it's over. Sara was in there,
        loving it obviously. It all happened
        so quickly. I'll just need some time
        to get my shit together, sleep this
        hangover off.

                MARC'S THOUGHTS
        And maybe never wake up?

                    CARA
        Fuck, that's rough.

Cara holds back her tears. She rolls her chair back to her desk
slowly.

                    CARA
                (From her desk)
        You know where I am right? You know,
        if you want to talk. Don't go quiet
        on me, this isn't the end. Start
        over tomorrow, yeah?

                    MARC
        Thanks.

Marc continues to pack his bag. He reaches for the framed
picture tucked behind his desk plant and glances down at the

picture of himself and the girl in the frame.

                    MARC
               (Under breath)
          I'm sorry.

END OF ACT ONE

ACT TWO

EXT. THE CITY   LATER THAT MORNING

Coming to terms with the morning's events, Marc meanders through the city slowly. He reaches for his cigarettes from within his jacket pocket, the packet's empty from the night before. He spots a nearby off licence and saunters to the entrance.

EXT. OFF LICENCE DOORWAY   MOMENTS LATER

As Marc approaches the doorway his attention is drawn to a HOMELESS MAN sitting outside the building. The Homeless Man, in his early sixties, is draped under a weathered sleeping bag. His hands are sealed around his mouth to keep warm.

> HOMELESS MAN
>
> Spare any change?

Marc eyes the Homeless Man's wristwatch.

> MARC'S THOUGHTS
>
> He has a nicer watch than I do.

> MARC
> (Awkwardly)
>
> Sorry mate, don't have any change on me at the moment. In the same boat as you now.

> HOMELESS MAN
>
> What's that supposed to mean?

> MARC
>
> Nothing, I don't know. Sorry.

Marc roots around in his trouser and jacket pockets for any loose change. He retracts his hands from his trouser pockets holding a lighter, a bottle top and an organ donor card.

> MARC

Organ donor card?

> HOMELESS MAN

Doesn't really mean anything unless you're dead, does it?

> MARC

You could have it for after I?

> HOMELESS MAN
> (Interrupting)

I don't want your organs. Keep it.

> MARC
> (Sheepishly)

OK, yeah, sure. I'll probably out live you any way I suppose.

> HOMELESS MAN

Yeah. Sure you will.

Marc re fills his pockets and enters the off licence.

INT. OFF LICENCE   CONTINUOUS

Marc walks straight to the alcohol fridges. He browses the cans and bottles quietly.

> MARC'S THOUGHTS

Is it too early for a drink?

He dismisses the fridge and turns towards the till. The SHOP KEEPER is elderly and silent.

> MARC

Hello, hi. Do you sell cigs here?
> (beat)

Of course you do, this is a fucking *Londis.*

An awkward silence.

> MARC

Sorry. Yeah, just a pack of *Sterling Blue,* please?

The Shop Keeper turns from the shop front and reaches for

the cigarettes from behind the counter. The Shop Keeper moves slowly. Marc peruses the spirits on a shelf above the counter. His eyes are drawn to an expensive bottle of whiskey coated in dust at the back of the shelf.

>   MARC
>   (Apprehensively)
>   And... uh, that as well.

He points to the bottle.

>   MARC
>   Yeah, the dusty one at the back.

Embarrassed by his purchases, Marc nervously clutches a multi pack of *KitKats* from the shelf behind him.

>   MARC'S THOUGHTS
>   *KitKats* to even it all out, this is
>   normal for a Tuesday morning, right?
>   Normal people buy dusty bottles of
>   spirit and tabs every day. Of course
>   this is normal.

The Shop Keeper places the whiskey onto the counter slowly and blows the dust from the neck of the bottle onto Marc's jacket. Still silent, the Shop Keeper counts the items into the till and points to the price on the register.

Marc reaches for his wallet and pays using his card. As the payment is accepted, he leaves for the exit.

>   SHOP KEEPER (O.S.)
>   (Faintly)
>   Excuse me.

Marc turns and re approaches the counter.

>   MARC
>   (Confused)
>   Sorry, did you say something?

They lock eyes as the Shop Keeper slowly slides an *Alcoholics Anonymous* leaflet towards Marc.

>   MARC
>   For me?

The Shop Keeper nods.

> MARC
>
> Oh, no. You see this is a... it's a
> gift, a birthday present. It's not
> for me.

> MARC'S THOUGHTS
>
> Liar.

Both stand in silence as Marc accepts the leaflet from the Shop
Keeper.

> MARC
>
> It's a gift, a bloody gift.

Marc turns and leaves in a hurry.

EXT. OFF LICENCE DOORWAY   CONTINUOUS

SFX: Off licence door closing.

Marc exits the off licence and stands within the doorway of the
shop. He crumples the leaflet into his jacket pocket. The Home
less Man is still sitting outside of the shop.

> MARC
>
> Here, got you these.

He hands him the *KitKats*.

> HOMELESS MAN
>
> No, you didn't. You needed to bal
> ance out that car crash with some
> thing sensible and the *KitKats* were
> the closest to the till. Don't lie
> to me son, I've seen that trick a
> million times.

> MARC
>
> Well, do you want them?

> HOMELESS MAN
>
> Obviously, I'm homeless.
>   (beat)
> You should get some help whilst you

still can.

                    MARC'S THOUGHTS
Life advice from *Oscar the Grouch*.

They both glance at the whiskey.

                    MARC
          (Frustrated)
     It's a gift, a fucking birthday
     gift.

                    HOMELESS MAN
     He slid you an *AA* leaflet, didn't
     he?

Marc closes his eyes and composes himself to avoid snapping back.

                    MARC
     Enjoy the biscuits.

Marc begins to walk away from the Homeless Man.

                    HOMELESS MAN (O.S.)
     What? No change either? Tight bas
     tard.

Marc continues walking.

INT. TUBE CARRIAGE   LATER

Marc stands with his head pressed against the carriage window of the tube. In one hand he holds the bottle of whiskey whilst his other hand holds onto a rail, he looks outward.

Deep in thought, he's processing the morning's events as a deep panic begins to overwhelm him. Marc unscrews the bottle and sips from the whiskey.

Feeling judgement on the tube from fellow commuters, Marc looks back out of the carriage window.

EXT. MARC'S FLAT   LATER THAT MORNING

Marc approaches the front door of his flat to find the front door ajar.

                    MARC'S THOUGHTS
          I don't think I left it open. Could
          I have? Surely not?

He grips the neck of the bottle of whiskey like a weapon and
enters through the open door slowly.

INT. MARC'S FLAT HALLWAY   CONTINUOUS

Marc enters the hallway slowly; he's expecting the worst. He
leaves the door open in case he needs to run out quickly and
begins to listen for intruders.

                    MARC'S THOUGHTS
          At least if I die now I don't need
          to look for a new job.
               (beat)
          Where the fuck is Spence?

                    MARC
               (Shouting, nervously)
          Spence? You in mate?

The flat is eerily silent, Marc glances into every room quickly
to find the flat is empty. As he turns to lock the front door,
SPENCE arrives with two bags of groceries in hand, he's shocked
to see Marc home so early.

                    MARC

          Spence?

                    SPENCE

          Marc?

                    MARC

          Why is the door open?

                    SPENCE

          Yeah, I just needed to go out and
          get a few things like bread, *Rizla*,
          a few bits. I lost my key a while
          back and didn't want to be locked
          out until you came home. Did you
          know it locks from the inside?

                    MARC
              (Frustrated)
         Yes? Of course I did.

                    MARC'S THOUGHTS
         No.

                    SPENCE
         Why you back so early? You're still
         fucked, aren't you? Have you slept?

Spence places his groceries onto the hallway floor.

                    MARC
         What? No, long story. I thought we
         were being robbed.

Marc takes off his jacket, he's relieved but not happy.

                    SPENCE
         I just needed to get a few things
         from the shop.

                    MARC
         Do you know how **stupid** that is mate?
         You left the flat wide open for **them**
         to come and take everything.

                    SPENCE
         Them?

                    MARC
         You know, the men, the robbers. I
         don't know, just anyone. It doesn't
         matter who. How many times have you
         done this?

                    MARC'S THOUGHTS
         Stupid question. Won't like the
         answer.

                    SPENCE
         A few times, whenever I've needed
         stuff... weed, cigs, milkshakes.

Marc's at boiling point. He glances downward towards Spence's groceries before recoiling.

>   MARC
>   (Jaded)
>   I need you to leave.

>   SPENCE
>   What? What the fuck are you talking
>   about? Don't joke about that.

>   MARC
>   (Seriously)
>   I'm sorry Spence. This isn't working
>   for me anymore.

>   SPENCE
>   (Worryingly)
>   Marc? Is everything OK mate? We can
>   get a key cut, I won't...

>   MARC
>   (Interrupting)
>   No, everything's **not** OK. I lost my
>   job today... I'm going to need to
>   lease the room out to somebody who
>   can pay rent.
>   (beat)
>   I'm sorry. I just can't afford to
>   pay for us both anymore.

Spence stands heartbroken, he picks up his groceries and shuf
fles beside Marc toward the spare room.

>   SPENCE
>   OK, yeah, sure man. I'll pack my
>   things and leave when you're at
>   group tonight.

>   MARC
>   I'm sorry mate, I just...

>   SPENCE
>   (Interrupting)
>   No, you're right. I've overstayed
>   my welcome and leaving the door
>   open was stupid, we could have been

robbed.

                    MARC'S THOUGHTS
I could have been robbed.

                    MARC
                 (Guiltily)
Look, you don't need to go straight
away...

                    SPENCE
                 (Interrupting)
I'll be fine.
                 (beat)
You need to look after yourself
though Marc. I'm telling you this
as your friend. I worry about you,
we all do. The way things are and
the way you're heading, it isn't
healthy.

Spence glares at Marc's bottle of whiskey.

                    SPENCE
                 (Concerned)
I should be putting you in the
recovery position in the event of
an emergency, not every Friday night
mate.
                 (beat)
I know it weighs on you, what hap
pened with... Heather.

                    MARC
                 (Interrupting)
Don't, just don't. This isn't about
her.

Both stand in silence before Marc turns into his bedroom and
slams his door shut.

SFX: Door slamming.

Spence stands quietly, he's heartbroken.

INT. BEDROOM   CONTINUOUS

Marc stands with his back pressed against his bedroom door; he begins to lower himself to the ground. He sits by the foot of the door. He unscrews the whiskey cap and takes a big mouthful.

SFX: *Spence packing his belongings.*

He continues to drink from the bottle as he reaches for his phone from his trouser pocket. He hovers his finger over calling HEATHER.

He scrolls further through his contacts and calls LIV.

SFX: *Phone dialling out.*

> LIV (V.O.)
> (Confused)
> Marc? What do you want?

> MARC
> (Into phone)
> Yeah, hi. How are you? Are you good?

> LIV (V.O.)
> Yeah, good. What do you want? We never call each other, this is weird.

> MARC
> (Into phone, with purpose)
> I know, weird right? I just thought maybe we could... do you want to come over later or something? Few drinks, maybe a takeaway? Film?

She holds for a moment.

> LIV (V.O.)
> (Reserved)
> Marc...
> (beat)
> We don't do that. I don't want to complicate things between us.

She can sense Marc is upset.

> LIV (V.O.)
> Look, any other night Marc. I'm not

feeling great   period cramps, or
else I'd have been there. Sorry.

> MARC
> (Into phone)

Yeah, of course, I know. Don't worry
about it. Hope you feel better,
sorry for calling.

SFX: *Dead phone line.*

Liv hangs up the call.

Marc takes a bigger mouthful from the bottle and stands to his
feet, he wobbles slightly. He removes his coat and throws his
work bag onto the bed before laying his head back onto the
pillow.

Marc takes a final sip before closing his eyes and passing out
fully clothed. A single tear rolls down his cheek. The camera
pans down to the crumpled *AA* leaflet on his bedroom floor.

END OF ACT TWO

ACT THREE

INT. THE COMMUNITY CENTRE   LATER THAT EVENING

Marc, still drunk, enters the community centre. He's late for group. Avoiding eye contact, he takes his jacket off and sits on an available chair within the circle.

> MARC
> (Interrupting)
> Sorry I'm late everyone and yes, I did forget the biscuits. I had them, fucking *KitKats* as well but gave them away so sorry about that.

SFX: Group moaning.

The GROUP LEADER turns to Marc.

> GROUP LEADER
> Wow, what an entrance.
> (beat)
> I think that's the most open you've been with us since you started Marc. Disappointing but thank you for being honest.

> MARC'S THOUGHTS
> A little on the nose but I'll let it slide.

> MARC
> (To the group)
> Sorry. Sorry everyone.

> GROUP LEADER
> Better late than never I suppose.
> (beat)
> We were just welcoming our newest member to the group. So, where were we?

> (beat)
> Ah yes, can we all give a big
> friendly group welcome to... Sara.

For the first time since sitting down, Marc raises his head and scans the room. There she is, sitting across from him, it's Sara. She's staring back at him in disbelief.

> MARC'S THOUGHTS
> (Franticly)
> This can't be real? I'm dreaming.
> Am I in hell? Is this hell? I gave
> *KitKats* to the homeless for fuck's
> sake.

Marc and Sara lock eyes. This is a new light for her, she's vulnerable. She waves awkwardly to the group before smiling anxiously back to Marc. He ignores her.

> GROUP LEADER
> As with all new members, we'd love
> to hear a little bit about yourself
> Sara and why you're here. That sort
> of thing. Only talk about things you
> feel comfortable about and remember,
> we're here to listen.

Sara etches forward, vulnerable, she inhales before sighing deeply.

> SARA
> (Anxiously)
> Hi, good evening, sorry was that
> really formal? Erm, I'm Sara... but
> you already knew that from before.
> (beat)
> Sorry, I'm nervous. I've never actu
> ally done anything like this before.

> GROUP LEADER
> You're OK. Take your time.

> SARA
> OK, yeah. Thank you.

> MARC'S THOUGHTS

Who the is this person? Where's the hatred and the malice?

> SARA

I'm Sara, I'm a middle manager at a... erm, it doesn't really matter what I do. I guess I'm here for a few reasons really. I've always strug gled with my confidence and being able to talk about my feelings. I hate being alone with my thoughts and I don't really like the person I've become. I nearly didn't come here tonight because I was embar rassed.

> GROUP LEADER
> (Sympathetically)

Why don't you like the person you've become? Who were you before?

> SARA

To be perfectly honest, I don't know. I don't understand why I'm feeling this way. I've dealt with these feelings, the self hatred and loathing for years. I just bury them until I'm occupied with something else.
> (beat)
I'm good at knowing when things are good and when they're bad.
> (beat)
They've been bad for quite a long time.

> GROUP LEADER

And is this the first time you've addressed these feelings? Tried to come to terms with them?

> SARA

Yeah... I've learned to put on a brave face at work, to my family, friends even. I'm afraid of my feel ings taking over fully and burning out. People wouldn't understand. I'm already hated at work as it is. It's easier to bury everything.

Marc acknowledges Sara.

> SARA
>
> Before I got my job I struggled, nearly did something stupid. I even planned it. I wrote a letter to my parents telling them it wasn't their fault and to remember me for me.
> (beat)
> I planned to hurt myself. Something I wouldn't come back from.

> MARC'S THOUGHTS
>
> Should have stayed in bed.

> SARA
> (Weeping)
>
> But I didn't, I couldn't do it. I never thought I'd be this lonely and isolated. I'm struggling.

She wipes back a tear with the sleeve of her jacket.

> SARA
> (Composing herself, sniffling)
>
> It's stupid and I don't know why I'm telling you this, but I recently baked a cake for a co worker on her birthday. Got up three hours before work to make it and she didn't even thank me, let alone taste it.
> (beat)
> Only one person did and I'm grate ful.

> MARC'S THOUGHTS
>
> Awful, awful cake.

> SARA
>
> Sorry. You didn't need to hear that.

It's stupid. I'm just grateful one person made an effort.

She glances thankfully to Marc.

> GROUP LEADER
>
> Thank you, Sara. I'm grateful for your honesty. I can't imagine how hard that must have been to talk about. We're to help and we'll support you in any way that we can. I'll catch you at the end of the group to discuss help and any professional options you might have available to you.

> SARA
> (Sniffling)
>
> Thank you.

INT. THE COMMUNITY CENTRE   END OF THE SESSION

The group session is wrapping up.

> GROUP LEADER
>
> I think we're just about out of time for tonight's session so thank you all for coming back. I look forward to seeing you again next week.
> (beat)
> **Oh!** Before you leave, has anybody seen or heard from Mary? I can't seem to get a hold of her.

The group falls silent.

> GROUP LEADER
>
> Not to worry, I'll see you all next week. Thanks again, and Marc, biscuits next week, please? You know we have a system.

> MARC
> (Bothered)
>
> Yeah, will do. Sorry.

The group stack their chairs and begin to funnel out of the community centre. Marc leaves promptly as Sara and the Group Leader can be seen talking in the background.

EXT. THE COMMUNITY CENTRE   MOMENTS LATER

Marc exits the community centre and reaches into his jacket pocket for his cigarettes, he lights one slowly. Sara exits the community centre and stands hesitantly behind Marc.

>   SARA (O.S.)
>   You've been drinking, haven't you?

Marc, still facing away from Sara, exhales deeply and turns unwillingly towards her.

>   MARC
>   (Under breath)
>   Better not bitter.

He snaps. He can't control it.

>   MARC
>   You don't manage me anymore, Sara.

She looks downward, guilty.

>   SARA
>   I'm sorry, I shouldn't have... I
>   just...

>   MARC
>   (Interrupting)
>   Just what?

>   SARA
>   (Abjectly)
>   It's nothing, sorry. I won't come
>   back next week, I didn't know you
>   came here.

She turns from Marc and walks away from the community centre into the darkness. He watches her leave; his guilt begins to mount.

>   MARC (O.S.)
>   (Shouting)

No... wait. I'm sorry.

Sara arcs back towards him.

>   MARC
>
>   Look, I had no idea. If it's any
>   consolation you did the right thing
>   coming here, these are good people.

She smiles with a genuine understanding and walks back towards him.

>   SARA
>
>   Thanks. I had no idea you were a
>   part of this, how long have you been
>   coming here?

>   MARC
>   (Awkwardly)
>
>   About six months now. I don't say
>   much, not fully opened up yet. Not
>   like you, that was... really good.
>   Shit, sorry, no, poor choice of
>   words. Not good but it was brave...
>   strong.

>   SARA
>
>   When I started, I couldn't stop. It
>   just kept coming out. Guess I've had
>   it bottled up for such a long time.

They begin to walk away from the community centre in the direction of the city. The atmosphere is awkward.

>   MARC
>
>   I've always hated Steph, always
>   found her very two faced.

>   MARC'S THOUGHTS
>
>   Just roll with it, don't bring up
>   the fucking cake again.

>   SARA
>
>   Trust me, I know what she's like.
>   She'll throw anybody under the bus.

                    MARC

Yeah, bloody **snake** in the stationery
cupboard.

                    SARA

What?

                    MARC

Just a... work joke.
     (beat)
Look, I don't know where my old
position stands but is there any
chance...

                    SARA
     (Interrupting)
No, Marc. I'm sorry but my hands are
tied. Even if I wanted to...

                    MARC
     (Interrupting)
OK, yeah, sure.

                    SARA

I wish things were different, I
really do, but I think we both know
this has been coming for a long
time.
     (beat)
There's a melancholy about you Marc,
it was starting to reflect in your
work... I know we don't work to
gether anymore and I know I'm not
your manager but as a group mem
ber to another, please look after
yourself.

                    MARC

It's hard.

                    MARC'S THOUGHTS

This is fine, I'm fine? I am not
fine.

                    SARA

> Just take some time. Get back on
> your feet, find out who you are
> again. Thank you for tonight, you're
> a good person.

EXT. THE CITY   LATER

Marc and Sara continue to walk through the city together. The conversation begins to end naturally. They arrive outside of The Priory, a pub Marc frequents. Their journey slows to a gradual halt.

> MARC'S THOUGHTS
> Don't do it.

> MARC
> (Signalling inside)
> Do you maybe fancy a drink for old
> time's sake?

Sara pauses to think about Marc's offer.

> SARA
> Fuck it. Yes, why not? I don't
> remember the last time I was invited
> to go for a drink.

> MARC'S THOUGHTS
> Act surprised.

> MARC
> Oh, really?

The atmosphere is still awkward, they both walk towards the entrance of the pub.

INT. THE PRIORY   CONTINUOUS

The inside of The Priory is small and busy but Marc and Sara are not deterred. They weave through the crowd before Marc squeezes into a space at the bar and tries to draw the attention of the barmaid. She's extremely busy.

As Marc waits to be served, he surveys the interior of The Priory for a table. He struggles to see through the busy crowd before sighting a brief gap towards the back of the pub. His eyes are immediately drawn to a table in the corner of the room. Upon further inspection, he spots Liv sitting in deep conversation with a good looking gentleman. He has his arm around her.

His gaze fixates for a moment longer than it should, the pub is too busy for Liv to notice him at the bar. He turns and faces Sara.

>   MARC
>   (Flustered)
>   This was a mistake. I have to go.

>   SARA
>   Marc? Is everything OK?

>   MARC
>   No. I'm sorry. I can't be here, not
>   right now.

He begins weaving back through the crowd towards the exit.

EXT. THE PRIORY   CONTINUOUS

Marc spills onto the pavement outside of the pub. He collapses back onto the wall of The Priory. One hand holds on to the exterior for support as the other clenches his chest. Short of breath, Marc begins having a panic attack as Sara rushes to join him.

>   SARA
>   (Concerned)
>   Are you alright? What happened in
>   there?

He struggles for air; words are escaping him.

>   SARA
>   Just breathe. Slowly. Keep breath
>   ing. I think you're having a panic
>   attack.

>   MARC
>   (Short of breath)
>   I feel like I'm dying.

Marc's breathing begins to slow as he composes himself gradually. He stands upright towards Sara as his breathing steadies.

> MARC
> Thanks. I have to go.

> SARA
> (Confused)
> Bye... then?

He turns from Sara and runs into the night.

INT. MARC'S FLAT HALLWAY   LATER THAT EVENING

Marc arrives back at the flat feeling sorry for himself. He closes the door quietly and leans back against the frame. He looks upward towards the ceiling; he closes his eyes. He's relieved to be home.

The flat is eerily dark. He walks towards the spare room to apologise to Spence.

> MARC
> Spence, mate...

He glares into the empty room; Spence has moved out.

> MARC
> ... I'm sorry.

INT. BEDROOM   MOMENTS LATER

Marc sulks into his bedroom and settles onto his bed. He seizes the expensive bottle of whiskey and finishes the last of it. The taste is harsh and Marc winces shortly after consuming the last of the spirit.

He reaches for his work bag thrown onto his bed from earlier in the day and clutches the framed picture from within. He places it on his bedside table and reaches for his phone with his other hand. He struggles to scroll through his contacts but locates Heather's name.

SFX: Phone dialling out.

Marc lays his head back and brings his phone to his ear. As the call dials through, Marc passes out before Heather finally answers.

> HEATHER (V.O.)
> This has to stop, Marc.

SFX: *Dead phone line.*

Heather hangs up.

CUT TO BLACK.

END OF EPISODE TWO

MELANCHOLY DAYS

Episode Three

ACT ONE

OVER BLACK.

SFX: Thumping dance music and inaudible shouting from club goers fade in gradually.

                    MARC (V.O.)
               (Shouting, slurring)
          Whiskey, straight.
               (beat)
          Yeah, whiskey.
               (beat)
          Just the house. Straight. A big one,
          double.

INT. NIGHTCLUB BAR   MIDNIGHT

MARC stands alone and inebriated at the bar of a busy night club. Leaning into the wooden panelling of the bar interior, he sways from side to side under the influence. His eyes struggle to adapt to the club's strobe lighting.

Marc attempts to weave his way back to the dance floor through the busy crowd. He shuffles difficultly until clashing and spilling his drink over a CLUB GOER's dress.

                    CLUB GOER
               (Shouting, angrily)
          Fucking hell. **Watch it!**

                    MARC
               (Slurring)
          Sorry... no, **you** watch it.
               (beat)
          Sorry, I'm, **I'm f fucked.**

                    CLUB GOER
          Fucking creep.

He continues to the dance floor.

QUICK MONTAGE:

INT. NIGHT CLUB DANCE FLOOR   CONTINUOUS

   Marc dancing alone in the crowd.

   Marc singing to the ceiling of the nightclub.

INT. NIGHTCLUB BAR   CONTINUOUS

   Marc downing several colourful shots, alone.

   Marc attempting to get the bartender's attention.

   Marc being ignored by the bartender.

INT. NIGHT CLUB TOILETS   CONTINUOUS

   Marc sniffing cocaine.

   Marc being sick with his head over the toilet seat.

END MONTAGE.

EXT. ALLEY OUTSIDE OF NIGHTCLUB   MOMENTS LATER

Hard cut to Marc being thrown out of the back door of the
nightclub by a muscular BOUNCER. Too inebriated to fight back,
he stumbles to his knees.

                    BOUNCER (O.S.)
          Fuck off and don't come back.

SFX: Door slamming.

Marc kneels momentarily before tilting his head back and look
ing up to the night sky.

EXT. DIMLY LIT ALLEY   LATER, THE EARLY HOURS OF THE MORNING

Marc stumbles home alone through the city. The city is quiet.
He takes a shortcut through a dimly lit alley and staggers into
an outdoor waste bin before slowing his speed to gather his
balance.

                    MARC
               (Slurring, singing)
          Walking home, alone. Home, alone.
          What's new... eh?

Marc falters further down the alley before reaching into his trouser pocket for his phone. In his unfortunate state, he struggles to unlock his phone and retires to the alley floor. He sits on a flattened cardboard box. It begins to rain. Marc manages to unlock his phone and looks at an old picture of himself and the girl from his picture frame. This is HEATHER.

> MARC
> (Slurring, to himself)

Sorry Heath Heather. My, my lovely, lovely Heather. I'm sorry. Not tonight.

He lays back onto the cardboard box and stares into the night. The world is spinning.

> MARC
> (Slurring, to himself)

Ah, fuck.

TITLES OVER BLACK: MELANCHOLY DAYS

SFX: Glass breaking and shattering.

INT. THE COMMUNITY CENTRE   THE FOLLOWING EVENING

SFX: Muffled conversation amongst group members.

Feeling sorry for himself and extremely hungover, Marc sits fragile in group the following evening. His arms are folded as one hand clutches an empty water bottle and the other his phone. His eyes are protected by a pair of darkly tinted sun glasses as he struggles to remain present with the session.

               NEIL
          (Fading in)
... And that's when she asked me to get tested for chlamydia.

              MARC'S THOUGHTS
          (Pained)
Head is pounding.
          (beat)
Did he just say chlamydia?

Dismissing NEIL with her hand, the GROUP LEADER stands from her chair.

              GROUP LEADER
OK... thanks for that, Neil. I'm glad your trip to the *London Eye* was...
          (beat)
... eventful. I'm happy things are starting to look up. She sounds... colourful.

              MARC'S THOUGHTS
Need to stop falling asleep in group.

               NEIL
Swings and roundabouts I suppose. I didn't enjoy the wheel that much. Just the sex.

              GROUP LEADER
          (Interrupting)
OK, Neil.

Bringing her hands together, the Group Leader steps into the group circle and addresses the room.

              GROUP LEADER
Well, I suppose that draws this week's session to a close. Are you sure there's nothing you want to

talk about this week Marc?

Marc has zoned out again. He returns to the room.

> MARC
> (Confused)
> What? Sorry. What did I miss?

> GROUP LEADER
> It's OK, Marc.
> (beat)
> Before you go, I need to speak to you at the end of the session if you don't mind hanging on after everybody's left?

> MARC
> Yeah, sure.

> MARC'S THOUGHTS
> I do mind. I want to go home.

> GROUP LEADER
> (To the group)
> Thank you all again for coming this week. If you could stack your chairs in the usual corner that would be excellent.

The Group Leader points towards the corner of the room as group members begin to stand and stack their chairs in an orderly fashion. Marc rises slowly, he's afraid of moving too suddenly.

> GROUP LEADER
> I'll be with you in a moment, Marc.

> MARC'S THOUGHTS
> I swear this is how most porn starts. Does she want to do porn with me? In my current state? No. She saw me sleeping, didn't she?

Group members begin to trickle out of the community centre. Marc stacks his chair quietly before checking his texts in the doorway of the community centre.

                    LIV (TEXT MESSAGE)
          Need to stay over. I'll come after
          work drinks at like 2? You'll be up,
          right?

He looks up from his screen and frowns.

SFX: Chair being stacked loudly, passive aggressively.

                    GROUP LEADER (O.S.)
          A little help would have been nice.

He looks over to the corner of the room.

                    MARC
                 (Apologetically)
          Uh, yeah. Sorry. Sorry about that. I
          think I'd have probably thrown up if
          I'd have lifted another chair.

                    GROUP LEADER
          Hungover again?
                 (beat)
          You look like shit.

He nods shamefully. The Group Leader approaches him slowly.

                    GROUP LEADER
          I know. You weren't fooling anybody
          tonight. Take the glasses off, this
          isn't America.

                    MARC'S THOUGHTS
          I wish it was. Anywhere but my body
          right now.

The Group Leader turns from Marc and signals towards a wooden
gymnastic bench at the end of the room.

                    GROUP LEADER
          Come, sit with me.

He follows a step behind her as they both sit down and face the
wall opposite. There's an awkward silence between them.

                    MARC'S THOUGHTS

If she starts singing, I'm going to kill myself.

                MARC

Look, if this is about the biscuits or sleeping in group then I'm sorry.

                GROUP LEADER
                (Confused)

What? No. It's not about that. I didn't know you were asleep in group.

                MARC
                (Uncomfortably)

I wasn't. I'm just one of those people who can sleep with their eyes open. It sneaks up on me and then I wake up and it's just... awkward. Can, can you do that? Sleep with your eyes open? Not many people can.

                MARC'S THOUGHTS

What the fuck are you talking about?

                GROUP LEADER

I don't think so. No. Anyway, that's not why I wanted to talk to you.

                MARC

Yeah, of course. Everything OK? Am I in trouble? Feels like I'm back in school.

                MARC'S THOUGHTS

Don't encourage the porn.

The Group Leader reclines back onto the bench. She's avoiding something.

                GROUP LEADER
                (Reflectively)

You know Marc, you've been coming to these sessions for six, almost seven months now. You haven't missed a single meeting since your first. No matter how hungover or beaten you've been feeling, you've always shown up.

                    MARC
Yeah... I guess?

                GROUP LEADER
But, as we both know, you haven't fully opened up to the group yet. You come, sit, and I like your con sistency, but you avoid talking to us. You just sit, often spaced out from the rest of the group.
        (beat)
This group and these people, we're a community. You can talk to us, we're like minded people, like yourself.

                MARC'S THOUGHTS
Am I being fired from here as well?

                GROUP LEADER
From what I've picked up on, I know there's a girl, or there was a girl involved.
        (beat)
Relationships are hard. I understand it can be difficult telling a room full of strangers about your life, especially if you're a private per son, but...

                    MARC
        (Interrupting)
I just, I guess, I don't want to be judged.
        (beat)
I sit in this room every week and listen to people crying about fights with their boyfriends, hear ing shitty stories about buying full fat milk instead of soya and how that made them feel suicidal, it's trivial.

(beat)
I keep coming back because it makes
me feel slightly better about my
self. That I don't feel the same way
these people do about things that
aren't problems because my problems
are real. It's selfish, I know, but
it helps me sleep at night knowing I
don't work myself up over fabricated
shit.

                    MARC'S THOUGHTS
Where did that come from?

                    GROUP LEADER
Wow. There it is.
     (beat)
That's the most I've heard you say
in six months Marc.

                    MARC'S THOUGHTS
Me too.

                    MARC
Yeah. I suppose.

                    GROUP LEADER
Thank you. Do you want to talk about
the girl?

                    MARC
No... not yet. I'm not ready. I'm
sorry, I can't.

                    GROUP LEADER
That's OK. We don't need to.

The Group Leader leans forward from the bench. There's still a
lingering discomfort about her demeanour.

                    GROUP LEADER
Thank you again truly for opening
up to me Marc but that wasn't the
reason I asked you to stay back
with me this evening.

He's puzzled.

> GROUP LEADER
>
> There's something important we need to discuss.

> MARC'S THOUGHTS
>
> Not the biscuits again, surely not?

> MARC
>
> OK? What's going on?

> GROUP LEADER
>
> I received a call this afternoon from Ascot Rehabilitation Centre. You know the one near the big *Costco*?

> MARC'S THOUGHTS
>
> Does she want me to go? Booked me a one way ticket to sober town? Career change maybe?

> MARC
>
> Not really but I've watched TV. I know what happens in a place like that. Straitjackets and pillow walls.

> GROUP LEADER
>
> Well, it was Mary on the phone.
>   (beat)
> You know Mary? With the twitch? Her oin addict? She was in recovery.

Marc remembers and nods back to her in agreement.

> GROUP LEADER
>
> She's not doing too well, Marc.
>   (beat)
> She tried to take her life two weeks ago.

> MARC
>
> Fuck. Sorry, didn't mean to swear.

I'm sorry to hear that. Is she OK?
Stable?

                    GROUP LEADER
She tried to overdose. She didn't
say with what, but an overdose is an
overdose.
          (beat)
She told me she'd been on a bender
and couldn't handle it anymore.

She hesitates and turns to Marc.

                    MARC
Why are you telling me this?

                    GROUP LEADER
Well, she told me her bender started
with drugs that you gave her.

Marc is taken aback by her accusation.

                    MARC
          (Panicked)
What? I didn't? I wouldn't!

                    GROUP LEADER
          (Interrupting)
Did you give her anything Marc? I
need you to tell me the truth. No
bullshitting.

                    MARC
I wouldn't... I, I didn't... I've
never even spoken to her let alone
given her anything.

Marc reaches for his chest and feels it tighten.

                    MARC'S THOUGHTS
Liv's missing gear.

                    GROUP LEADER
Are you clean?

                    MARC'S THOUGHTS
Tell her you are. You're a good

liar. You need to lie.

MARC

No.

The Group Leader withdraws from Marc. She sighs deeply and thinks about Marc's admission. The silence feels like an eternity.

MARC

Look, I didn't...

GROUP LEADER
(Interrupting)
Marc, I'm afraid I have no
other option but to believe
Mary.

MARC
(Desperately)
I didn't give her anything. I
wouldn't lie about something like
this.

GROUP LEADER

Please don't make this worse for
yourself. Why would she lie to me?
(beat)
Your actions go against everything
we stand for here. You are actively
putting yourself and other group
members at risk by showing up to
these sessions with drugs. You're
already a risk turning up to these
meetings drunk or hungover.

Marc begins to tear up, he's speechless.

GROUP LEADER

Please don't return to future meet
ings Marc.

MARC

I need these sessions.

GROUP LEADER

If you'd have opened up to us sooner Marc, we'd have been able to help you or prevent something like this happening. Sara told me you lost your job.

                    MARC
She fucking fired me!
        (beat)
I didn't do this, please listen to me. This is the only thing that...

                GROUP LEADER
        (Interrupting)
Take care of yourself, Marc. Seek the professional help you need. Make good choices. You have options.

Marc stands from the bench and races for the door of the community centre.

                GROUP LEADER (O.S.)
Marc? Marc?

EXT. THE COMMUNITY CENTRE   CONTINUOUS

Marc exits the community centre and spills onto the street clutching his chest. He struggles to breathe and gasps for air. He reaches for the wall of the community centre to stabilise himself.

Marc is having a panic attack.

END OF ACT ONE

ACT TWO

INT. BEDROOM   THE FOLLOWING MORNING

Marc wakes in his bed alone, he's hungover, again. He turns his head towards his bedside table but struggles to keep his eyes open. His bedside table is littered with empty cans of lager. He closes his eyes.

>   MARC
>
>   Urgh.

SFX: Toilet flushing.

Marc sits to attention.

>   MARC
>   (Unsure)
>   Spence?

His bedroom door opens, LIV enters. She's fully clothed and glares down towards Marc in disappointment.

>   LIV
>   What? Spence?
>   (beat)
>   How fucked were you last night?

>   MARC
>   (Disappointed)
>   Oh yeah, it's you.

>   LIV
>   Who's Mary? Is she your mum? You
>   kept talking about her last night,
>   it was weird. The crying as well,
>   you did that **a lot**.

He remembers his conversation with the Group leader.

>   MARC
>   Oh, fuck off.

>   LIV

What did you say?

>   MARC

Nothing, I'm just hungover.

>   MARC'S THOUGHTS

And wishing you'd just admit you're
sleeping with other people.

>   LIV

Sure. Look, I need to go. I need
to... wash my hair?

>   MARC

You don't need to make excuses. You
can just go.

>   LIV

Good. Yeah, I just need to get away
from this bedroom. The smell and
whatever quarter life crisis you're
having... it's not good for me.

She reaches for her bag and exits his bedroom without saying
goodbye.

SFX: Front door slamming.

>   MARC
>   (Sarcastically)

Great.

Marc lays back onto his bed and brings a pillow to his face. He
screams with everything he has into the pillow before launch
ing it across the room. He lies quietly, still.

SFX: Text message notification.

Startled by the notification, Marc reaches for his phone under
the sheets of his bed.

>   CARA (TEXT MESSAGE)

*See you tonight. 8:30 at mine. Bring
a bottle.*

Marc throws his phone back onto the bed and reaches for a second pillow. He repeats the process of screaming into the second pillow and launches it across his bedroom.

                    MARC'S THOUGHTS
          Cara's birthday. Can't miss it, can
          I? No, can't. Need to show everyone
          I'm fine and not an alcoholic re
          cluse. Maybe Spence will be there?
          It's fine, I'm fine.

INT. KITCHEN   LUNCHTIME

Marc enters the kitchen and opens the fridge. The fridge consists of a browning banana, two cans of lager, a takeaway pizza box and an open tin of cat food.

                    MARC'S THOUGHTS
          I don't even have a fucking cat.

He reaches for a can of lager and the pizza box before closing the fridge and tossing the cat food into the bin.

                    MARC'S THOUGHTS
          Hair of the dog and pizza crusts for
          lunch?
                    (beat)
          It is truly disgusting being me.

INT. BEDROOM   MOMENTS LATER

Marc slumps back onto his bed. Holding the pizza box in one hand and his lager in the other, he sits and thinks.

SFX: Text message notification.

He places the pizza box onto the bed and reads the text.

                    LIV (TEXT MESSAGE)
          *Left my Oyster card at yours, bring
          it to Cara's tonight.*

He glances over to notice the card resting on his bedside table.

                    MARC'S THOUGHTS
          Eat the cat food, make yourself

sick. Never have to leave the flat
again... fool proof.

EXT. CARA'S HOUSE   EVENING

SFX: Loud music inside the house.

Marc stands before CARA's front door, she lives in a three
story house share. He's debating leaving. In one hand he
clutches a cheap bottle of red wine, in the other hand he car
ries a crate of lager.

> MARC'S THOUGHTS
>
> Could leave the bottle by the door
> and run? Could probably throw it
> through the window and blame it on
> *Hermes*.

SFX: Knocking on door.

He knocks on the door and Cara answers immediately. His eyes
are drawn to the oversized birthday badge on her chest. Cara is
already tipsy.

> CARA
> (Slurring)
>
> About time, you shit! Why were you
> lurking outside for so long?

> MARC'S THOUGHTS
>
> She's already fucked.

> MARC
>
> Suppose I've got nothing better to
> do these days you big... fucking...
> **twat**.

Both stand in the doorway in awkward silence.

> MARC'S THOUGHTS
>
> Is this how we greet each other
> outside of work? Maybe she'll kick
> me in the shin and steal my wallet.
> Why not stab me?

> CARA
>
> Come in, come in. Let's get you a

drink. It's my birthday after all.

They both sheepishly enter the party.

INT. CARA'S HALLWAY   CONTINUOUS

Both enter into the hallway of the house. The party is in full swing.

>   MARC
>   Here, got you this.

He hands her the cheap bottle of red wine and she examines the label.

>   CARA
>   (Patronisingly)
>   Bless you. You shouldn't have... you
>   didn't need to get me anything!

>   MARC'S THOUGHTS
>   But you'd have crucified me if I
>   didn't.

>   MARC
>   It's nothing, don't mention it.

>   CLARA
>   (Interrupting)
>   Does that say 'Slauvignon'?

>   MARC
>   (Confidently)
>   Yeah, I think it's new, a new wine.
>   A bloody French one. You know what
>   they're like.

>   MARC'S THOUGHTS
>   The strongest garage wine for under
>   a fiver.

Cara places the bottle on the radiator in the hallway politely and smiles thankfully. They both walk into the kitchen.

INT. CARA'S KITCHEN   CONTINUOUS

Marc and Cara enter the kitchen and Marc rests his crate on the table. The kitchen is small and cramped with party guests. Marc tears open the crate aggressively with both hands and reaches for a bottle. He opens the bottle with his teeth.

Uncomfortable with Marc's bottle opening technique, Cara's friends leave the kitchen.

>   MARC
>   (To Cara)
> What did I do?

>   CARA
>   (Flustered)
> Don't pull your caveman schtick here
> Marc, this is a classy event. Use a
> bottle opener next time, please?

She hands him a bottle opener from the cutlery draw. Marc holds his hands up apologetically.

>   MARC
> Best behaviour.

>   CARA
> Thanks. Before I forget, I need to
> talk to you about something.

>   MARC'S THOUGHTS
> Why does everybody need to talk to
> me about something?

>   MARC
> What's up?

>   CARA
> I've got a friend who works over at
> Lawson's. The advertising firm?
>   (beat)
> Anyway, we were talking over drinks
> the other night...

>   MARC'S THOUGHTS
> Also code for I slept with him.

>   CARA
> And he told me they have an opening

at the moment. So, I mentioned you
were looking for work and he wants
me to email over your CV. They'll
consider you for an interview, if
you're interested?

                MARC
           (Thankfully)

Oh, God. Yes, please? That would be
amazing. Thank you.

Liv enters the kitchen. She's glued to her phone and doesn't
notice Marc and Cara talking in the corner of the room.

                LIV

Where's the guy opening bottles with
his teeth? I fucking love that
trick.

She scans the kitchen and is again disappointed to see Marc.

                LIV

Oh, it's just you.

                MARC

You'll have to pay to see that trick
again.

The room falls awkwardly silent. Marc's joke hasn't landed.

                MARC

Nice to see you too by the way.
Here, got your *Oyster* card. You
staying again tonight?

She snatches the card from Marc and leans in with a genuine
worry whilst shaking her head.

                LIV
           (Whispering)

Just don't bring us up again or that
we're fucking. Don't ruin this for
me.

                MARC
           (Whispering, confused)

Ruin what?

Behind Liv enters the good looking gentleman from Episode Two. He's carrying an expensive bottle of champagne. This is BENJAMIN, he's extremely handsome and the tallest man in the room. He's never paid for his own phone bill and holidays in the south of France on his father's dime. He's never Ben, always Benjamin.

                    BENJAMIN (O.S.)
          Liv? Are you in here darling?

                    MARC'S THOUGHTS
          I hate that I know exactly what's
          going on here.

Benjamin enters the kitchen and extends his arm around Liv.

                         LIV
                    (Nervously)
          Everyone... I'd like you to meet
          Benjamin.
                    (beat)
          My, erm, boyfriend.
                    (beat)
          Benjamin... this is everyone.

                         CARA
          Glad you could make it Benjamin,
          pleasure. It's Cara by the way, it's
          my birthday.

She points to her badge.

                         MARC
                    (Disinterested)
          Yeah, hi Ben, or whatever. It's
          Marc.

                    BENJAMIN
          It's Benjamin.

                         MARC
          Yeah OK, Ben.

                    BENJAMIN

It's Benjamin.

Benjamin brushes Marc off and hands Cara the champagne.

> BENJAMIN
> This is for you. Happy birthday,
> thanks for having us.

> MARC'S THOUGHTS
> Bet he didn't buy that from a
> garage.

Benjamin squeezes Liv tighter and kisses her head. She looks to Marc uneasily.

> CARA
> You guys! Thank you so much. You
> really didn't need to.
> (beat)
> It's the expensive stuff as well!

> MARC'S THOUGHTS
> I could stab myself and that would
> probably be better than this is. I'm
> her, aren't I? The other woman? Her
> bit of rough on the side? It can't
> get any worse than this?

Liv turns to Cara.

> CARA
> Oh, thanks again for letting us know
> about the opening. Sara's going to
> interview Benjamin next week.

> MARC'S THOUGHTS
> It just got worse.

> CARA
> Anytime. I think Steph's in the liv
> ing room, you should introduce Ben.

> BENJAMIN
> It's Benjamin.

Liv and Benjamin shuffle out of the kitchen into the living room. Marc turns to Cara furiously.

                    MARC
                (Angrily)
What the fuck Cara? You got him an
interview for my old job?

                    CARA
No, Marc. He applied for the posi
tion and Sara gave him an interview.
Everything isn't always about you.

                MARC'S THOUGHTS
It is.

                    MARC
                (Bothered)
Sure. Look, I don't feel great. I
might head off, get an early night.

                    CARA
Don't go. Come on, it's my birthday.
Just go out there and mingle with
people, you might meet someone.

                    MARC
Fine. I'm only staying because it's
your birthday.

                    CARA
Just don't bring the room down, you
can be a bit of a bummer. Just don't
talk about killing yourself or how
hungover you are.

                MARC'S THOUGHTS
Killing myself could be your birth
day present.

                    MARC
I'll need a few more of these before
I mingle.

Marc reaches for two bottles from his crate on the table.

                    CARA
                (Sarcastically)

If it helps.

Marc opens both bottles with his teeth and downs the first drink before emptying the second bottle in succession. He reaches for a third before Cara confronts him.

>   CARA
>   (Disbelief)
>   What have I literally just said?

>   MARC
>   (Gassy)
>   Shit. Sorry. Not with my teeth, got
>   you.

INT. CARA'S LIVING ROOM   MOMENTS LATER

Marc enters Cara's living room and scans for someone to mingle with. Knowing nobody at the party, except Liv, Cara and Steph, he shuffles through the crowd to the living room window. He nudges through the crowd awkwardly.

>   MARC
>   Sorry. Sorry mate.
>   (beat)
>   Just need to squeeze by, great
>   party, right?

>   MARC'S THOUGHTS
>   Who are all of these people?

INT. CARA'S LIVING ROOM WINDOW   CONTINUOUS

Marc squeezes into a tight corner by the living window and looks out onto the road.

>   MARC'S THOUGHTS
>   Finish your drink, smile for a
>   photo, go for a piss and leave. Why
>   did I wait until now to need a piss?

He looks back into the crowded room.

>   MARC'S THOUGHTS
>   Fuck walking through that again.

Marc glances back out of the living room window. Walking

towards the front of the house is SPENCE and MIKE.

Mike is a go getter; he works in a bank and is an old friend of Spence's from university. Obsessed with the idea of rekindling the 'uni gang', he's actually quite a nice guy.

> MARC'S THOUGHTS
> Spence? He came.
>> (beat)
> And Mike. Bedwetter.

Marc looks away from the window as if to have not seen them approach. He pretends to look at his phone before attempting to shuffle back through the crowd to the kitchen.

INT. CARA'S KITCHEN   MOMENTS LATER

Marc, Spence and Mike stand cramped in the corner of the kitchen.

> SPENCE
> Yeah, I'm holding up in Mike's spare room at the moment.

> MARC'S THOUGHTS
> (Angrily)
> Fucking Mike.

Marc plays it cool and reaches for another drink.

> MARC
> Oh, yeah. Great news. Yeah, I'm happy for you mate. Feels like a good fit.

> MARC'S THOUGHTS
> Nothing feels good anymore.

> MIKE
> (Overjoyed, a brag almost)
> I've been telling Speno to move in for months now and he finally said yes. We've had such a laugh... just like old times.

> MARC
> Speno?

> SPENCE
> (Displeased)

Speno.

> MIKE

Just the boys, the old gang back
together.

> MARC'S THOUGHTS

We had a gang Mike, and you were
definitely not a part of it.

Throwing caution to the wind, Marc opens yet another bottle
with his teeth.

> MARC
> (Faking)

Sounds great fellas, really does.
How the fuck are you anyway Mike?
How long has it been?

He pats Mike on the shoulder causing him to stumble backwards
into a cupboard.

> MIKE

Well, now that you ask, still at the
bank. A couple of promotions here
and...

> MARC
> (Interrupting)

Yeah, yeah. That's great mate. Here,
I think Cara needs a drink. You
wouldn't let the birthday girl go
thirsty, would you?

Marc hands him Benjamin's expensive champagne and gestures to
the crowded living room.

> MIKE
> (Confused)

But I've never met Cara?

> MARC

You'll work it out mate, smart
banker like you. Go on, big birthday

badge. You can't miss her.

Mike shuffles into the crowded living room out of shot. Marc corners Spence.

> MARC
>
> Finally. You have to move back in mate. Fuck Mike. I bet he has you eating rice pudding and watching *Pointless*.
> (beat)
> That's not you. I know the real you. Cigarettes out the kitchen window and porn in the sleeping bag. Move back in?

Spence thinks about it.

> SPENCE
>
> No, Marc. You were right. I was in the way, not paying any rent, eating your food and feeding the stray cat.

> MARC'S THOUGHTS
>
> It all makes sense now.

> MARC
>
> I didn't want you to move out. It was just the heat of the moment. You can move back in and we'll go back to normal. We'll get some more keys cut for when you inevitably lose yours, fill the fridge back up.
> (beat)
> What do you say?

> SPENCE
>
> I can't. I'm doing OK now Marc. I've got an interview at the bank. It's just admin, entry level but it's something. I'm going to save for my own place.

> MARC'S THOUGHTS
>
> He's excelling because he's away from me.

Marc finishes another bottle. He's intensifying with every drink.

> MARC
> (Genuinely)
> That's great mate. I'm happy for you. You deserve it.

> SPENCE
> Thanks. I appreciate that. I know we left things weirdly, but I hope you're OK.

Marc puts on a brave face.

> MARC
> Who? Me? Yeah, of course. Got an interview next week, advertising if you can believe it? Been back to the gym, bulking the **fuck out**. A real self improvement vibe over at the flat.

> MARC'S THOUGHTS
> Crying in the bath and a cat food dinner.

> SPENCE
> Sounds like it's all coming to gether.

Both stand in the moment, it's clear they're both masking their unhappiness.

> MARC
> Yeah, got all the cat food I need.

> SPENCE
> (Puzzled)
> What?

> MARC
> Was it not?
> (beat)
> Nothing mate, just a... a funny

party joke.

Both sip their drinks awkwardly.

>   MARC
>   Anyway mate, I'm going to go for a
>   slash. I'll catch you after.

Marc signals to the downstairs bathroom.

>   SPENCE
>   (Interrupting)
>   Yeah, sure. I'll be here.

Marc extends his fist out for a fist bump whilst Spence goes in for a high five and the pair mangle hands in the middle. Shrugging the awkwardness off, Marc walks out of shot to the bathroom.

END OF ACT TWO

ACT THREE

INT. CARA'S DOWNSTAIRS BATHROOM   LATER

Marc stands motionless in front of a hanging mirror in Cara's downstairs bathroom. The tap runs cold over his hands. As he stares at his reflection, he acknowledges how drunk he's becoming.

SFX: *Knocking on the bathroom door.*

Marc snaps out of his trance and to attention.

> LIV (V.O.)
>
> Are you nearly done in there? I need to piss!

> MARC
> (Shouting back)
>
> Yep. One second.

Marc takes one last look at himself in the mirror. He turns the cold tap off and splashes his face. He closes his eyes before sighing deeply. He seizes his bottle and exits the bathroom.

INT. CARA'S HALLWAY   CONTINUOUS

Marc enters the hallway from the downstairs bathroom to find Liv and Benjamin waiting for the toilet.

> LIV
>
> What were you doing in there? Why is your face so sweaty?

Marc rubs the cold water from his forehead.

> MARC
>
> It's just cold water. Look.

He extends his hand to show them.

> LIV
> (Offended)

What? I don't want to touch your
sweaty hands.

> BENJAMIN

Yeah, not cool mate.

> MARC

Yeah alright, Ben.

> BENJAMIN

It's Benjamin.

> MARC

All yours.

Liv and Benjamin enter the downstairs bathroom and shut the
door behind them.

SFX: Bathroom door closing.

Marc stumbles through the hallway and back into the kitchen.

INT. CARA'S KITCHEN   CONTINUOUS

Spence has since departed from the kitchen as Marc hovers in
the same corner. He reaches for the last bottle in his crate.
Cara enters and approaches him.

> CARA
> (Concerned)

Who are half of these people?
> (beat)

You good?

She glances down at the empty crate.

> MARC

I'll be OK. I'm OK.

> CARA

You're throwing them back. Just,
maybe slow down a bit, please?

> MARC

I'm, I'm fine. It's a great party.
Am I sweaty? Liv thinks I'm sweaty.

> CARA

A little.
>> (beat)

Slow down for me, yeah?
>> (beat)

Some guy brought me Ben's champagne earlier. Mike, was it?

> MARC
>> (Slurring)

It's Benjamin.

> CARA

Oh, I thought he was called Mike?

> MARC
>> (Slurring)

He is. I told him to bring you a drink. I tried to convince Spence to move back in.
>> (beat)

I hate that guy. **Mike**.

> CARA

You hate everyone. He's quite good looking. Single?

> MARC
>> (Slurring)

Not you as well. Spence should still be living at mine. **Fucking Mike**.

> CARA

OK, calm down. He's fine. He seems nice. Here, have some water.

Cara pours Marc a glass of water. Marc shrugs her off, he's riled.

> MARC
>> (Slurring, angered)

I'm fine.
>> (beat)

I don't know, I just need to tell Mike to fuck off and then I'll go.

Cara blocks his path.

>   CARA
>   (Seriously, pleading)
>   Don't do this Marc. Don't fucking
>   ruin my birthday party. You can ruin
>   your own life on your own terms but
>   not here, not now. This is my night.

There's a glimmer of composure in his eyes.

>   CARA
>   I don't want to have to look after
>   you again, especially not tonight.

>   MARC
>   (Slurring)
>   OK. OK, Cara.

He glances over from the kitchen into the crowded living room.
He spots Spence, Mike, Liv and Benjamin in conversation, they
all laugh simultaneously.

>   MARC
>   (Slurring, distressed)
>   What are they saying about me?

Marc loses his composure and hurtles into the living room.

INT. CARA'S LIVING ROOM   CONTINUOUS

Marc wades through the busy crowd in the living room, his
frustration has turned into rage. His eyes are locked onto
Mike. He flies into Liv and knocks her drink over Benjamin's
shirt. Liv falls to the floor.

Marc balances himself before continuing towards Mike. Benjamin
stands in his way. Marc gestures towards Liv on the floor.

>   MARC
>   (Slurring, angered)
>   And you can fuck off too. Fuck you.
>   You know she's still fucking me,
>   right?

>   BENJAMIN

What? Liv?

> LIV
> Ben. I can explain...

Taking a moment to process the news, Benjamin scowls at Liv before turning and lunging for Marc in a fit of rage.

SFX: Party guests scream.

Benjamin punches Marc twice. His first punch catches Marc's eye and his second grazes his nose. Too inebriated to fight back, Marc falls back into the crowd and holds his face. Benjamin leaves the party furiously before anybody has a chance to intervene.

> MARC
> (Not alright)
> I'm alright.

Spence rushes to Marc's aid and picks him up from within the crowd. Marc clasps the bridge of his nose as it bleeds profusely. Cara hands him a tea towel for the blood. Liv stands to her feet in tears. Marc begins to sober up.

> LIV
> What the **fuck** have you done Marc? What is your fucking problem?

> MARC
> What? He went for me. He's an animal.

> LIV
> (Interrupting)
> Fuck off. Don't you **dare** act like you weren't coming over here to start a fight with someone. We all saw the look in your eyes.
> (beat)
> You're not right up here Marc.

She points towards his head.

> LIV
> Clean yourself up and get some fuck ing help.

The party stands shocked at the events of the last five minutes. Liv leaves the party in tears.

>   SPENCE
>   (Awkwardly)
>   She's right mate. I'll make sure she
>   gets home safely. Keep holding that.

Spence points to Marc's nose and leaves the party after Liv. Marc stands alone in the living room holding the bridge of his nose, he's embarrassed. He turns to Cara.

>   MARC
>   You were right, I did ruin your
>   birthday.

>   CARA
>   (Fed up)
>   Just go. **Please**.

He leaves through the kitchen and slams down the bloody tea towel onto the table next to his empty lager crate. As he exits the room, he seizes Benjamin's champagne for Cara and leaves the party disgraced.

EXT. DIMLY LIT STREET   MIDNIGHT

Marc sits alone on the curb of a dimly lit street. His shirt is bloodstained as he continues to drink from the bottle of champagne. He reaches for a cigarette and fails to light it. He reaches for his phone from his trouser pocket. His screen has cracked in the altercation with Benjamin, but he can still use it functionally.

>   MARC
>   (To himself)
>   Fuck.

He brings the phone to his ear.

SFX: *Phone dialling out.*

>   HEATHER (V.O.)
>   (Tiredly)
>   Marc?
>   (beat)

>   What do you want?

He tries to act sober.

>   MARC
>   (Into phone, slurring)
>   No, no. Please don't hang up. I need
>   to, need to talk.

She can sense he's not well.

>   HEATHER (V.O.)
>   I won't hang up. Talk.

>   MARC
>   (Into phone, slurring)
>   I'm not good. It keeps bleeding.

>   HEATHER (V.O.)
>   (Urgently)
>   What's bleeding? Are you OK? Where
>   are you?

>   MARC
>   (Into phone, slurring)
>   It's just my nose. I don't know
>   where I am. What am I doing?

>   HEATHER (V.O.)
>   I don't know Marc. You tell me. Are
>   you hurt?

>   MARC
>   (Into phone, slurring)
>   You should see the other guy... he's
>   fine.

>   HEATHER (V.O.)
>   Marc, you need to stop. Stop calling
>   me like this. We can't do this every
>   week. It's not fair. Tell me where
>   you are, I'll book you an *Uber*.

Marc begins to sob.

>   MARC
>   (Into phone, slurring)

I'm sorry for what I did to you. It should have been me. I need to come home.

She pauses, suspended in disbelief.

> HEATHER (V.O.)

Tell me where you are.

> MARC
> (Into phone, slurring)

It doesn't matter. I'll see you soon.

Marc hangs up the phone abruptly. He clambers to his feet and takes a final sip from the champagne bottle before throwing it into the distance.

SFX: Bottle smashing.

EXT. LIV'S HOUSE   LATER

Marc arrives outside of Liv's house.

SFX: Phone dialling out.

She doesn't answer his initial call, he tries to call again.

SFX: Phone dialling out.

> LIV (V.O.)

Go home, Marc.

> MARC
> (Into phone, slurring)

It's me, Marc.

> LIV (V.O.)

Yeah, I know.

> MARC
> (Into phone, slurring)

I'm outside. Can I come in?

> LIV (V.O.)

No. Go home.

> MARC

> (Into phone, slurring)
> I forgive you.

> LIV (V.O.)
> Excuse me?

Marc glances up to her bedroom window. Liv opens the curtains slightly and peers down towards him in the street.

INT. LIV'S BEDROOM   CONTINUOUS

> MARC (V.O.)
> (Slurring)
> I forgive you. For using me. Let's start over. Clean s slate.

> LIV
> (Into phone)
> Go home, Marc. Get some sleep. You can't come up. I can't see you right now. Not like this.

> MARC (V.O.)
> (Slurring)
> P Please?

> LIV
> (Into phone)
> No. Good night.

She hangs up and draws the curtains.

EXT. LIV'S HOUSE   CONTINUOUS

Marc watches Liv's curtains close. He stumbles into the night.

INT. LIV'S BEDROOM   CONTINUOUS

Liv reopens her curtains ever so slightly and watches Marc descend into the darkness. She turns from her window into the bedroom and glances down to her bed regretfully.

The camera pans towards Spence in her bed asleep, he's unclothed.

> LIV
> (Under breath)

Fuck's sake.

INT. BEDROOM   LATER

After stumbling home, Marc has passed out onto his bed. He lays unconscious and fully clothed; his room is dimly lit by his unlocked phone screen. Fast asleep, the camera pans from Marc towards his bedside table and the unlocked phone screen.

His screen displays a booking confirmation.

PHONE NOTIFICATION

Please travel safely on your Cross Country journey.

CUT TO BLACK.

END OF EPISODE THREE

MELANCHOLY DAYS

Episode Four

ACT ONE

OVER BLACK.

SFX: *The rattling of a quiet train carriage fades in.*

SFX: *The TRAIN CONDUCTOR checking passenger tickets.*

> MARC
> (Nauseously)
> Fucking hell.

INT. TRAIN CARRIAGE   MORNING

MARC sits alone with his head leant against the window of the train carriage. He's extremely hungover, the shaking of the carriage isn't helping. Sporting a swollen black eye from the night before, he's partially covered the bruise with his pair of tinted sunglasses. It's evident he's not in a good way.

The Train Conductor approaches. He's stocky and humourless.

> MARC'S THOUGHTS
> Show your tickets. No sudden move
> ments. Do **not**, I repeat, do **not** be
> sick.

The Train Conductor arrives at Marc's seat.

> TRAIN CONDUCTOR
> Tickets please.

Marc reaches into his trouser pocket delicately for his ticket.

> MARC
> Yep. One sec.

The Train Conductor can smell the alcohol on Marc's breath. He rolls his eyes and shares with Marc an all too familiar look of disappointment.

> TRAIN CONDUCTOR
> (Irked)

You should have had them ready for checking when you boarded the train.

                    MARC
Yeah. I said one second pal.

                MARC'S THOUGHTS
If the carriage shakes anymore I'll have last night's drink ready for him.

Marc continues to route around in his pockets. He begins to fluster.

                TRAIN CONDUCTOR
When you're ready sir. I have the remainder of the train's tickets to check.

                    MARC
                (Flustered)
Yeah, I heard you the first time mate.

Marc finally locates his ticket and hands it to the Train Conductor. The Train Conductor checks the ticket and shakes disapprovingly towards Marc. There's a problem.

                TRAIN CONDUCTOR
            (Looking at the ticket)
I'm afraid you're sitting in the wrong seat. This is an aisle ticket and you're currently sitting in a window seat.
                (beat)
I'm going to have to ask you to move into the aisle, please?

                    MARC
What? There's nobody sitting in the window seat. It's empty. The **train** is empty.

                TRAIN CONDUCTOR
                (Robotic)
As the conductor of this vessel, I

have to ensure all passengers are following the rules and are sitting in their assigned seats. I took an oath.

                    MARC

An oath? What are you talking about? This isn't *Game of Thrones*. Your job is to literally check tickets and extort those who don't have one. Un like **me**, who has a paid for, in ad vance, ticket.

                MARC'S THOUGHTS

Stop moving. For the love of God, please **stop**.

                TRAIN CONDUCTOR
                    (Robotic)

If you don't move to your assigned seat then I'm afraid I'll have no other option but to ask you to exit the train at the next station.

                MARC'S THOUGHTS

He doesn't have the power or the balls.

                    MARC

Listen, mate, I know you're only doing your job and you're doing it tremendously, but this is overkill. All of it. The train is quiet. I'm not disturbing anyone, we're good here.

The Train Conductor stands over Marc, he folds his arms.

                    MARC

Fine. **Fine.** I'll move if it means you'll fuck off.

                TRAIN CONDUCTOR
                    (Sarcastically)

Thank you very much sir.

To show his dissatisfaction, Marc stands and edges over into the aisle seat in frustration.

> MARC
>
> But as soon as you **piss off** down the train, I'll...

Marc stops himself; he can feel the sudden urge to throw up. He relieves himself from his seat and scurries past the Train Conductor and down the carriage to the onboard toilet.

> TRAIN CONDUCTOR (O.S.)
>
> You'll what?

INT. TRAIN CARRIAGE TOILET   CONTINUOUS

Marc bursts into the carriage toilet and notices the toilet is clogged with tissues. His only other option is to throw up into the sink. After spewing into the sink, he glances into the mirror above. His glasses fall into the pool below. This is a new low for Marc.

Feeling relieved and disgusted in himself, he examines the black eye Benjamin gave him the night before. His heart sinks.

> MARC'S THOUGHTS
>
> This... is as low as it gets.

Marc wipes down his glasses with toilet roll. He straightens his outfit and splashes his face with cold water.

SFX: The Train Conductor continuing to check passenger tickets.

INT. TRAIN CARRIAGE   MOMENTS LATER

Marc exits the toilet. The Train Conductor passes him to get through to the adjoining carriage.

> TRAIN CONDUCTOR
> (Smirking)
> You deserve that... dick.

TITLES OVER BLACK: MELANCHOLY DAYS

SFX: Glass breaking and shattering.

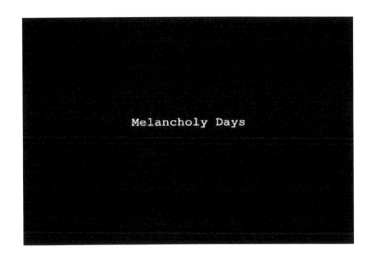

Melancholy Days

EXT. TRAIN STATION PLATFORM   LATER THAT MORNING

We hard cut to Marc sitting on a bench at the train station. Still cleaning the sick from his glasses, he reflects briefly. The station is quiet. He looks up to the electronic notice board above.

> ELECTRONIC NOTICE BOARD
>
> *The next train will arrive in 7 minutes.*

> MARC'S THOUGHTS
>
> Could just go back. Could go any where really. Nobody knows I'm here.

He knows he can't leave after coming all this way. He looks down the platform and then up to the roof of the station. He reaches for his phone from his trouser pocket. His phone screen is smashed but functional.

> MARC'S THOUGHTS
>
> For fuck's sake.

SFX: Phone dialling out.

> MUM (V.O.)
>
> Marc?

He holds before answering.

>   MARC
>   (Into phone)
>   Yeah... it's me.

>   MUM (V.O.)
>   Is everything OK? You don't sound
>   too good?

>   MARC
>   (Into phone)
>   I'm fine. Just hungover. Rough
>   night.

>   MUM (V.O.)
>   You're always hungover when you call
>   me.

>   MARC
>   (Into phone)
>   Yeah, I know.
>   (beat)
>   Look, I called because I'm here. I'm
>   home.

>   MUM (V.O.)
>   What? You're home? Why didn't you
>   tell us sooner? We could have picked
>   you up from the station.

>   MARC
>   (Into phone)
>   Can you come and get me?

>   MUM (V.O.)
>   (Concerned)
>   Okay Marco. Won't be long.

>   MARC
>   (Into phone)
>   Nobody calls me...

MUM hangs up.

SFX: Dead phone line.

>   MARC
>   (Into phone, sarcastic
>   ally)
> Brilliant.

EXT. TRAIN STATION CARPARK   LATER

Marc stands in the train station carpark. Mum pulls into the carpark and stops her car in front of him. Mum is in her early sixties, she's loud and kind but fiercely protective. The car rolls to a gradual stop before she departs from the driver's seat.

>   MUM
>   (Concerned)
> What happened to your eye?

>   MARC
> It's nothing Mum, wrong place, wrong
> time. I'm fine.

They hug in the carpark, it's a touching moment.

>   MUM
> Is this why you've come home Marco?

>   MARC
> No, I just needed to get out of the
> city. Nobody calls me Marco anymore,
> Mum.

She walks around to the driver's seat.

>   MUM
>   (Whispering, looking
>   around)
> Are you in trouble?
>   (beat)
> Do you owe people money?

>   MARC'S THOUGHTS
> Who does she think I am?

>   MARC
> What? No. I came home to see you and
> Dad.

Mum pauses with concern before they enter the car.

> MUM
>
> If you say so.
>   (beat)
> Are you going to be OK getting in
> the front? There's space in the back
> if that's better for you? You know
> after the...

> MARC
>   (Interrupting)
> The front's good.

Mum smiles back at Marc kindly. They both climb into the car.

INT. MUM'S CAR   MOMENTS LATER

> MUM
>
> You don't seem yourself Marco.

> MARC'S THOUGHTS
>
> Marc.

> MUM
>
> I know when you're lying to me.
> You've been doing it since you were
> born.

Mum starts the car and exits the train station carpark.

> MARC
>
> I'm OK. Everything's fine, promise.
> Can we just... drive?

> MUM
>
> Your Dad and I, we just worry about
> you. After everything that happened,
> we...

> MARC
>   (Interrupting)
> I'm **fine**.

> MUM
>
> OK, OK. I'll stop asking.

She tries to lighten the mood.

> MUM
>
> Don't forget to say hello to your brother when we get back.

Marc rolls his eyes.

> MARC
> (Snapping back)
>
> He's not my brother. He's a fucking dog. He's more like an ornament that shits himself three times a day.

> MUM
> (Displeased)
>
> Really? Do you need to swear?

> MARC
>
> Yes, really. Gets my point across.

The car falls silent. Marc holds onto his seatbelt tightly. Mum can sense his apprehension of being in the front seat of the car.

> MUM
>
> I'll take it nice and easy, there's no rush.
> (beat)
> He's missed you.

Marc loosens his grip on the seatbelt.

> MARC
>
> I've missed him too, and Dad.
> (beat)
> All of you.

> MUM
>
> It's nice to have you back Marco.

> MARC'S THOUGHTS
>
> Marc.

> MUM
>
> The house hasn't been the same since

you left.

              MARC
I had to go, you...

              MUM
     (Interrupting)
OH! Mrs Davies died at number
eleven, did I tell you? Terrible
thing it was, pneumonia took her.
Bless her heart.

              MARC
     (Unmoved)
I mean it'd been coming. She was
ninety seven.

              MUM
     (Shocked)
Marc!
     (beat)
That's awful. A bit of compassion
for the dead please?

              MARC
Yeah, I know. She was getting on is
all I'm saying. It's not surprising
news. People die when they're old.

              MUM
People are living longer these days,
life is winning.

              MARC
I guess but the woman had lived
through a world war and a recession.
She'd done her fair share of living.

              MUM
It wouldn't kill you to think of
somebody else other than yourself
for a change.

              MARC
It's sad... I know it is. It's just
not a surprise to me. She was shaky

at the best of times.
(beat)
At least this means she won't be
bringing around a tray of jellied
meat this Christmas. Silver linings
I suppose.

                    MUM

Hmm.

INT. MUM AND DAD'S KITCHEN   LATER

Marc and Mum enter the kitchen. They're greeted by GRAHAM
(Marc's brother). Graham is a grey Pomeranian, aged seven, he
also goes by Gray. Marc bends down to greet him.

                    MARC

Gray! Hello boy.

                    MUM

Told you he's missed you.

                    MARC

He's fatter than last time. What are
you feeding him?

He strokes Gray softly before standing and helping himself to
a glass of water.

                    MUM
               (Sarcastically)

No, **you** help yourself, Marc. I
didn't want a drink anyway.

DAD follows Gray into the kitchen. He's in his early sixties
and retired. Emotion is something he struggles with but he's
working on it.

                    DAD

Marco, how are you son?

He pats Marc on the back which propels Marc forward spilling
his glass of water over Gray.

                    MARC
                 (Reeling)

It's just Marc these days, Dad.

Marc turns to Dad. Dad notices his black eye.

> DAD
>
> Christ, what happened? That's a
> beauty.

Marc reaches for a tea towel. He begins to dry Gray.

> MARC
>
> Wrong place, wrong time.

> DAD
>
> You don't need to lie to us son.
> What are you caught up in this time?
> Drugs?
>   (beat)
> It's not drugs, is it? Stupid boy.
> What are you playing at getting in
> volved with drugs?

> MARC'S THOUGHTS
>
> Not drugs but unemployment? De
> pression? Drunk dialling? Take your
> pick.

Marc turns to both Mum and Dad. He raises his hands as if to
surrender.

> MARC
>   (Convincingly)
> Not caught up in anything. I think I
> deserved it this time.

> DAD
>   (Concerned)
> What could you have possibly done to
> deserve this?

> MARC
>   (Feeling sorry for him
>   self)
> No, I did deserve this. I drank
> too much and have to suffer the
> consequences.
>   (beat)

I was a dick.

Marc reaches for his bag and hands Mum the tea towel. Dad feels awkward.

>   DAD
>
> Well, I hope you managed to get a
> few licks in at least?
>
>   MARC'S THOUGHTS
>
> Floored it and lost the use of my
> limbs.
>
>   MARC
>
> Yeah, one or two. It was only a
> scuffle. People have probably al
> ready forgotten about it.
>
>   MARC'S THOUGHTS
>
> Like *Swine Flu* or *Nine Eleven*.
>
>   MUM
>
> You're here now though, it'll be
> nice having you home Marco.
>
>   MARC'S THOUGHTS
>
> Marc.
>
>   MUM
>
> Go and get yourself cleaned up. You
> don't smell particularly fresh. I'll
> stick the kettle on.

Marc nods back to Mum. He leaves the kitchen.

INT. MUM AND DAD'S STAIRWELL   CONTINUOUS

Marc begins to climb the stairs slowly; he stops to look at a large picture frame of Gray hanging on the wall of the stairwell. The frame is substantially bigger than the one next to it of him. Marc can overhear Mum and Dad talking between themselves in the kitchen.

>   DAD (O.S.)
>   (Whispering)
>
> Did he tell you why he came home?

> MUM (O.S.)
> (Whispering)

No, he just said that everything was fine.

> DAD (O.S.)
> (Whispering)

You know he'd only come home if things were bad.

> MUM (O.S.)
> (Whispering)

I know. It's been years since we've seen him. I wonder if he'll see her.

> DAD (O.S.)
> (Whispering)

I hope so.

> MUM (O.S.)
> (Whispering)

I'll talk to him.

Marc continues up the stairs quietly and enters his old bedroom.

INT. MARC'S OLD BEDROOM   CONTINUOUS

Marc perches on the end of his bed and delicately pokes his black eye. He looks around his room in silence before sobbing to himself quietly.

END OF ACT ONE

ACT TWO

INT. MUM AND DAD'S KITCHEN   LUNCHTIME

Marc, Mum and Dad are sitting at the kitchen table having lunch. The atmosphere is sombre and more awkward than any of them want it to be.

> MUM
>
> Any plans whilst you're home?

> MARC
>   (Interrupting)
> The garden looks tidy.

> MUM
>
> Sorry.

> MARC
>
> Sorry.

They both sip their coffee in tandem.

> MARC
>
> Not really. Might see Dylan?
>   (beat)
> I'll be out of your hair tomorrow.

> DAD
>
> You can stay as long as you need to, this is still your home. Are you back in the office on Monday?

> MARC
>   (Hesitantly)
> I'm on holiday until Wednesday.

> MARC'S THOUGHTS
>
> And then indefinitely after that.

> MARC

I don't think I'll be here long.
It's just nice to get away from the
city.

> MUM

And how is work? Is your manager
still giving you a hard time?

> MARC

Work is work. It keeps the lights
on, fuels my hobbies.
> (beat)
She's not as bad these days.

> DAD
> (Unsure)

And what are your hobbies? What do
you get up to down there?

> MARC'S THOUGHTS

Cigs and binge drink.

> MARC

You know... just the usual. Friends.

> MARC'S THOUGHTS

I have absolutely no hobbies or
friends.

> MARC

Yeah, friends. So many bloody mates
in the city. We go out... do stuff.
I just see them most of the time.

> MARC'S THOUGHTS

Yeah, just see them leave Cara's
party ashamed to know me.

Mum and Dad look at each other worryingly. The atmosphere
shifts from sombre to concern.

> MUM

Marco...

> MARC'S THOUGHTS

Marc.

                    MUM

You'd tell us if something was
wrong, wouldn't you? I'm worried
we're going to lose you again.

                    MARC

You're not going to lose me. I've
told you, I'm good. Work's fine,
life's good.

                    MARC'S THOUGHTS

Liar.

Marc forces a smile, it's painful.

                    MUM

It's just... we haven't seen or
heard from you in months. Your
father and I know you're busy with
work in the city and that life
moves... differently there. Faster.
        (beat)
But you can always come home when
it gets too much. We're so proud of
you and how well you picked yourself
back up after everything.

                    DAD

So proud.

                    MUM

But, when you show up like this,
unannounced. It worries us. We don't
want to be overbearing and since it
happened, we know being away from
here was the best thing for you but
we...

                    MARC
        (Interrupting, snapping)
I'm **OK!** Look, I took a beating and
whether or not I deserved it, it
happened. I've moved on from it.
Let's just drop it, yeah?

> DAD
>
> OK son. We'll leave it there.

> MARC
>
> Thank you.

The atmosphere is sombre again. Marc tries to hurry the conversation on.

> MARC
>
> Yeah, so Dylan. Might see if he's about for a drink later at The Crown.

> DAD
>
> You should. He always asks after you when we've seen him.
> (beat)
> Do you think you'll see...?

Dad can't say her name. Marc looks away from the table, he's avoiding that conversation.

> MARC
>
> Yeah. Maybe. I'll just...

> DAD
> (Interrupting)
> Oh! Did Mum tell you about Mrs Davies at number eleven?

Marc rolls his eyes.

SFX: Gray barks loudly.

> DAD
>
> Terrible thing it was.

EXT. OUTSIDE OF THE CROWN   EVENING

We cut to Marc standing in the doorway of The Crown, his former local pub. Feeling anxious about going inside, he hasn't visited in two years and fears he'll bump into people from his past. He finishes his cigarette and throws it onto the floor.

He considers leaving and begins turning before being approached

and startled by DYLAN behind him. Dylan is everybody's child
hood friend who never left their hometown. He's a local plumber
with the beer belly to match, a weekend warrior in his own
right, he'll never live anywhere but here.

> DYLAN
> (Overexcited)

Marco!

> MARC'S THOUGHTS

Marc.

> MARC
> (Forced excitement)

Dylan!

The pair perform an uncomfortable high five/handshake medley
that turns into a forced hug.

> MARC'S THOUGHTS

He's gained so much weight.

> DYLAN

What the fuck happened to your eye?
Is everything alright? It's great to
hear from you mate. Didn't know you
were back in the area.

> MARC

Yeah, I'm good tha...

> DYLAN
> (Interrupting)

Tell me inside. Let's get a drink
first.

> MARC

Lead the way.

> MARC'S THOUGHTS

Fucking finally.

Dylan enters the pub first. Marc inhales deeply and follows
behind.

INT. THE CROWN   CONTINUOUS

The pair enter The Crown. All eyes are drawn to their arrival, this is hell for Marc. As they shuffle through the crowd, Marc recognises old school friends. Dylan greets them all, he's all too familiar with the clientele of the pub. They approach the bar; Marc keeps his head down.

> DYLAN
> (Excitedly)
> What are you having mate?

Marc scans the bar, he's extremely uncomfortable.

> MARC
> Look, I don't think this was a very good idea. I'm still hanging from last night.

> DYLAN
> Nonsense. I'm not having that. We never get to see each other. I haven't seen you in two years, this is long overdue. You might perk up after a drink, you always used to.

> MARC
> Fine, sure. Let me get these though, what are you having?

Marc waves over the attention of the BARMAID.

> DYLAN
> She knows what I'm having, just say it's for me and she'll know what to do.

> MARC
> OK? Sure. Go find us a table?

Dylan shuffles into the crowd and finds them a booth in the corner of the pub. The Barmaid approaches Marc.

> MARC
> Hey, yeah, Dylan's usual please? He said you'll know what that is?
> (beat)
> And for me, just a pint of the IPA

and a double house whiskey please?

>   BARMAID
Do you want ice in the whiskey? Any
mixer? It's free.

>   MARC
No. Thanks.

The Barmaid begins pouring their drinks, she pours Marc's
whiskey first. He almost snatches it from her hand and downs
the drink. She is not impressed. Marc tilts his head back and
closes his eyes, he needs this.

INT. THE CROWN (BOOTH)   MOMENTS LATER

Marc slumps into the booth. Dylan takes his drink and smiles
thankfully towards him.

>   DYLAN
Must have needed that drink, eh? No
shot for me?

>   MARC
>   (Confused)
Oh. Yeah, that. Been a long day.
Sorry.

>   DYLAN
They always are mate.

There's an awkwardness about their meeting.

>   MARC
>   (Lifting the mood)
I didn't know your 'usual' was half
Guinness, half cider. That's appal
ling.

>   DYLAN
Yeah, it's a modern play on a snake
bite. I think they call it a black
velvet in Ireland. You should be on
this.

They both sip their drinks.

                    MARC

Disgusting.

                    DYLAN

So...

                    MARC

So?

                    DYLAN

So... are you going to tell me what
happened to your eye? Come on Marc,
we've been best friends for twenty
years and you can barely string a
sentence together. It's only me.

Marc remembers his black eye, he touches it, it's still sore.

                    MARC

Sorry.
     (beat)
Yeah, this? It was just a scuffle at
a party, nothing too intense. Some
dickhead fancied a go really.

                 MARC'S THOUGHTS

You were the dickhead and you lost
the fight.

                    DYLAN

The city man, fights and knife
crime. Part of the reason I stayed
here. Home comforts and that.

                 MARC'S THOUGHTS

Yeah, that's the reason.

                    MARC
     (Shrugging it off)
It'll heal, these things happen.
     (beat)
How are you? Work OK?

                    DYLAN

They always do mate, it's good to

have you back. Work's good, no real
news in the plumbing game but I've
got my own company van so can't com
plain really.
>(beat)
You ever think about moving back up
here? It's not been the same since
you left. When you moved away it all
felt real... had to grow up and star
working.

>>>MARC
>>>(Reserved)

I think about it sometimes. I don't
know, I don't belong here anymore.

There's an air of regret about Marc, Dylan can sense it.

>>>DYLAN

Yeah, of course. You have to do
what's best for you, whatever that
is. You know I've been trying to get
Heather down here for months.
>(beat)
Hey! We could text her now, tell
her you're here. I think we could
squeeze her in at the end of the
booth, you know with the...

>>>MARC
>>>(Interrupting)

No, Dylan. I don't think that's a
good idea, I think I'll be heading
off soon anyway. I'm shattered.

>>>DYLAN
>>>(Disheartened)

Sure. Do you two keep in touch? Al
ways thought you two were endgame.

Marc reaches for his chest; his anxiety is back.

>>>MARC
>>>(Lying)

Yeah.
>(beat)

We talk every now and again.

Marc's glass is empty as Dylan finishes his drink. Dylan col
lects the empty glasses and stands from the booth.

> DYLAN
>
> It's my round. Don't go anywhere
> mate. We've got loads to catch up
> on. Same again? What is that? IPA?

> MARC
>
> Erm, yeah. Thanks.

Dylan leaves the booth and walks out of shot towards the bar.
Marc still feels as though he is being watched, he avoids look
ing outward from the booth. His breathing begins to increase,
he feels as though he might have another panic attack. He needs
to leave immediately.

Marc stands from the booth and runs for the exit of the pub
holding his chest. Dylan watches Marc leave. His eyes roll in
anticipation as he continues to order at the bar. He knows Marc
won't be back.

> DYLAN
>
> Scratch that, it's just my usual.

EXT. THE CROWN   CONTINUOUS

Marc spills out of The Crown's doorway and onto the road
outside of the pub. He stands still and embraces his panic at
tack; he tries to settle his breathing.

> MARC
> (Short of breath)
>
> Fuck. Why now?

Marc's breathing slows gradually. He begins walking home. He
can't face returning to the pub.

INT. MUM AND DAD'S KITCHEN   LATER THAT NIGHT

Marc enters Mum and Dad's kitchen quietly; he doesn't want
to wake them. Still reeling from his panic attack, he pours
himself a glass of water and sips it slowly. Dad enters the
kitchen, Gray follows.

                    DAD
Thought I heard you come in.

                    MARC
Sorry. I tried to be quiet. Didn't
want to wake you.

                    DAD
You didn't son, your mother clocks
off early these days whilst I'm up
watching the *Netflix*.

                MARC'S THOUGHTS
The *Netflix*.

                    MARC
OK, good. Watching anything inter
esting?

                    DAD
            (Interrupting)
Sit with me. You fancy a beer?

Dad gestures to the kitchen table.

                MARC'S THOUGHTS
Don't seem too keen.

Marc pauses.

                    MARC
Yeah. Why not?

Dad reaches into the fridge and pulls out two bottles of lager.
They both open their bottles with their teeth.

                    DAD
Best trick I ever taught you that.

They discard their bottle tops onto the table and sip in
tandem.

                    DAD
I'm sorry about earlier   the *Span
ish Inquisition* from your mother.
She just worries about you is all.

>   Hell, I worry about you son. You
>   don't talk to us as much as you used
>   to.
>   (beat)
>   I know you're busy with life and
>   with your work...

>   MARC
>   (Interrupting)
>   I lost my job, Dad.

Dad sits back in his chair. He sips from his beer.

>   DAD
>   (Unsurprised)
>   I know.

>   MARC
>   (Surprised)
>   What? How did you?

>   DAD
>   They took your picture off the com
>   pany website last week.

>   MARC
>   Oh. I see.

>   DAD
>   You've been so quiet, I've been
>   trying to keep an eye on you from a
>   distance to make sure you're OK.
>   (beat)
>   I thought the computer was on the
>   fritz or I'd broken the website, but
>   this makes more sense.

>   MARC
>   Dad, I...

>   DAD
>   (Interrupting)
>   Why didn't you tell us sooner Marco?

>   MARC'S THOUGHTS
>   Let it slide, we're having a moment.

                    MARC
        I was embarrassed. I didn't want you
        to worry any more than you already
        do, it's unnecessary stress. You
        don't need it in your lives.

                    DAD
        We **do** worry, it's our job to worry.
        What about group? Are you still
        going to group?

Marc tries to save face.

                    MARC
                (Sparingly)
        Yes. Still going to group. Every
        week.

                    MARC'S THOUGHTS
        But just not this week. Or next. Or
        after that.

                    DAD
        And the drinking? Is it bad again?

Marc's vulnerable, reality is hitting him hard.

                    MARC
        No.

                    MARC'S THOUGHTS
        Yes.

He breaks.

                    MARC
        Yes... I can't get her out of my
        head. What happened at the festival.
                (beat)
        I can't block it out or forget about
        it. I don't sleep anymore unless
        I've had a drink.

Dad begins to understand, he's heartbroken to see Marc this
way.

> DAD
>
> Marc. I had no idea. I'm sorry, I shouldn't have.

He glares at Marc's beer.

> MARC
> (Interrupting)
>
> It's fine, Dad.

> DAD
>
> Here I am offering you a beer. It was stupid of me.

> MARC
>
> No, it wasn't.
> (beat)
> I'm sorry, Dad. For everything. Being quiet, the radio silence, everything.

> DAD
>
> You should go see her. She needs to hear this from you.

> MARC
>
> I know.

> DAD
>
> Please start letting us in Marco. If not for me then for your mother. You know she misses talking to you.

> MARC
>
> I will, I promise.

> DAD
>
> I'll keep this between us until you're ready to tell your mother. Until you're back on your feet.

> MARC
>
> Thanks Dad.

Marc stands from the table and walks over to the sink in the kitchen. He drains the remainder of his beer and leaves Dad alone in the kitchen. Gray follows Marc.

END OF ACT TWO

ACT THREE

EXT. HEATHER'S HOUSE   MORNING

Marc stands on the footstep of HEATHER's front door. He's apprehensive, afraid of what's waiting for him on the other side of the door. He taps his thigh with his left hand and hovers over the doorbell with his right before ringing it.

>   MARC
>   (Under breath)
>   Better not bitter. Better not bit
>   ter.

SFX: *Doorbell chime.*

The wait for someone to answer feels like an eternity, Marc considers leaving before HEATHER'S MUM answers the door.

SFX: *Door opening.*

Heather's Mum is both tightly wound and a loose cannon. She hates Marc.

>   MARC'S THOUGHTS
>   Fucking hell, here we go.

>   HEATHER'S MUM
>   What are you doing here, Marc?

>   MARC
>   (Nervously)
>   I need to speak to her. To Heather,
>   sorry. Is she in?

>   HEATHER'S MUM
>   You know better than anyone she
>   doesn't go anywhere. She doesn't
>   have anything to say to you. **We**
>   don't have anything to say to you.
>   (beat)
>   You shouldn't have come back here.

                    MARC

I just need to...

                    HEATHER'S MUM
                (Interrupting)

So you finally got what's coming to
you then, did you?

                    MARC

Excuse me?

She points to his black eye. His head sinks as he tries to hide
his bruise.

                    MARC

You're right. This was a bad idea.
I'm sorry to have bothered you...

                    HEATHER (O.S.)
                (Interrupting)

Marc?

Heather calls Marc out of shot. Marc's head lifts anxiously.

Heather is beautiful and delicate; her voice is soft spoken.
Her beauty complements her kind nature but most people notice
her wheelchair first. She's Marc's first love and the girl in
his framed picture.

Heather approaches the door slowly in her wheelchair. She's
equally as shocked and as anxious to see Marc as he is to see
her.

                    MARC
                (Feebly)

Heather. I need to speak to...

                    HEATHER'S MUM
                (Interrupting, to
                Heather)

I can tell him to leave. He doesn't
need to be here.

                    MARC'S THOUGHTS

You'd get a kick out of that,
wouldn't you?

                    HEATHER
          No, it's OK Mum. I'm glad he's here,
          we have things we need to talk
          about.

Heather's Mum looks back towards Marc from Heather, he's still
standing in the doorway.

                    HEATHER'S MUM
               (To Marc)
          Five minutes. That's it. Then you're
          gone.

She backs away from the door slowly and into the house. She
leaves Heather and Marc staring at one another awkwardly in
the doorway.

                    MARC
          So...

INT. HEATHER'S BEDROOM   MOMENTS LATER

Heather's bedroom is on the bottom floor of the house. Her
bedroom has been converted from the family living room, it's
large and cosy but it's not a bedroom. Marc stands uncomfort
ably by the door, he's unable to bring himself to enter fully.

                    MARC'S THOUGHTS
          Say something.

                    MARC
          You've changed bedrooms.

                    MARC'S THOUGHTS
          Not that.

Heather sits expressionless.

                    HEATHER
          I had to. Can't really get up the
          stairs anymore.

Marc avoids eye contact. He's uncomfortable but he knows he has
to be here.

                    MARC

> (Regretfully)

Oh, yeah. Of course. Sorry. Stupid comment.

                    HEATHER

Dylan text me last night. He said you were back and that you ran away from the pub?

                    MARC

Yeah, I...

                    HEATHER
                    (Interrupting)

And your eye? What is going on with you?
> (beat)

Why are you here Marc?

Marc finally joins her and perches on the end of her bed.

                    MARC
                    (Voice breaking)

I don't think I'm very well.
> (beat)

I'm sorry I haven't been back sooner.

                    HEATHER
                    (Irritated)

I think you lost the right to worry about seeing me when we broke up after... this.

She signals to her chair.

                    MARC

I'm sor...

                    HEATHER
                    (Interrupting, angrily)

Don't you dare. You didn't **then** and you aren't going to **now**. It feels like a lifetime since it happened. Since you left me in that car.
> (beat)

I don't get angry at you anymore.
I can't afford to. This chair is a
constant reminder of you... of what
happened.

                    MARC
              (Interrupting)
Heather, listen, I...

                    HEATHER
              (Interrupting, snapping
              back)
No, **you** listen to me for once. It
has to stop. All of it. The calls,
the texts when you're shit faced, I
can't do it anymore. You can't grow
a conscience at the end of a bottle.
It doesn't work like that.

She lowers her voice and tries to compose herself.

                    HEATHER
I have to try and at least make
something of my life in this chair.

Marc sits in silence.

                    MARC
We should never have gone to the
festival.

                    HEATHER
You're right. Do you have any idea
why I agreed to go with you in the
first place?

                    MARC
              (Puzzled)
Why?

                    HEATHER
I was terrified. Terrified you were
going to kill yourself. The drink
ing, the drugs, the way you were
heading, I wanted to help you. Be
there to save you from yourself.

> (beat)

But you nearly killed me instead.

They're both crying now.

                    MARC

I didn't mean to.

                  HEATHER

I know you didn't. I know you loved
me, but you couldn't switch it off.
That side of you. I don't think
you'll ever be able to.

                    MARC

I'm trying.

                  HEATHER

I love you, Marc, I think I'll
always love you regardless of every
thing we've been through. You were
the love of my life and I know deep
down that's the reason I keep an
swering your calls... but we can't
keep doing this anymore. This isn't
real. We're not real.

> (beat)

You need to move on, the guilt is
killing you. I hate you for what you
did but I need to release you from
whatever hold I have over your life.
You need to let it go.

> (beat)

I should loathe you and sometimes
I fucking do with all my being but
it's not worth us both feeling like
this anymore.

                    MARC
> (Broken)

I can't sleep. I play it over and
over in my mind. Running away from
the car, leaving you.

                  HEATHER

>   That's not my problem anymore, Marc.
>   (beat)
>   You should leave now. Please don't
>   call me again.

He wipes the tears from his eyes and stands shaken.

>   MARC
>   (Sniffling)
>   Yeah. Ok.

>   HEATHER
>   Please leave me now... don't come
>   back here.

He turns to Heather's bedroom door.

>   HEATHER
>   And please stop drinking?

>   MARC
>   Yeah. I'll try.

Marc opens the bedroom door and stands in the doorframe.

>   HEATHER
>   You'll be OK Marc and so will I.
>   You need to start living your life
>   again.

He smiles back at her apologetically and leaves.

EXT. THE TRAIN STATION CARPARK   AFTERNOON

Mum's car arrives at the train station carpark. Mum, Dad and Marc all exit the vehicle.

>   MUM
>   It's been nice having you back
>   Marco.

>   MARC'S THOUGHTS
>   Marc.

>   MUM
>   We just wish you could have stayed
>   longer.

>   MARC

> This was...

>   MARC'S THOUGHTS

> Emotionally draining?

>   MARC

> ... nice. We'll plan ahead next
> time. I'm sorry it's been so long.

Mum hugs Marc, it's another touching moment.

>   DAD

> Look after yourself, be safe in the
> city and keep it in your pants son.

>   MARC

> Sorry? What was that?

>   DAD

> Keep it in your pants. Just take it
> easy, OK?

>   MARC

> Yeah. Will do?

Dad hugs Marc quickly, it's a fumbled embrace, awkward almost.

>   MUM

> They'll be OK at work with that?

She points to his black eye.

>   MARC

> Oh, yeah. I'll just tell them I
> walked into a cupboard or something.

>   MARC'S THOUGHTS

> Or Benjamin's fists.

>   MARC

> Thanks again for having me, I love
> you.

>   MUM

> Love you too.

Dad nods acceptingly towards him. He can't say it back but there's a mutual understanding between them. Marc turns and walks into the train station.

INT. TRAIN CARRIAGE   LATER

In sheer contrast to the beginning of the episode, Marc sits in the window seat of the train carriage with a new sense of purpose. Feeling a weight lifted, he glances out into the dis tance hopefully.

SFX: Phone ringing.

Marc reaches into his pocket for his phone and answers the call. It's a withheld number.

> MARC
> (Into phone)

Hello?

> CALLER (V.O.)

Hello, is that Marc?

> MARC
> (Into phone, awkwardly)

Yes. It is he speaking. Sorry. Yes, it's Marc.

> CALLER (V.O.)

Hello, my name is David and I'm calling from Lawson's Advertising. We were wondering if you'd be inter ested in coming in for an interview next week?

CUT TO BLACK.

END OF EPISODE FOUR

MELANCHOLY DAYS

Episode Five

ACT ONE

OVER BLACK.

SFX: Coffee shop interior. Coffee machines frothing and inaudible conversation between customers.

> CARA (V.O.)
> You ruined my **fucking** birthday, Marc.

INT. COFFEE SHOP   EARLY MORNING

MARC and CARA are sat opposite one another in two excessively large armchairs by the toilets of the coffee shop. Both have a coffee each. The shot hard cuts to a remorseful Marc. He's dressed in a suit and tie; his black eye is fading. The coffee shop is loud and busy.

> MARC
> Look, Cara, I'm s...

> CARA
> (Interrupting)
> I asked you to slow down but you didn't listen. You really fucking embarrassed me.
> (beat)
> Why am I here?

> MARC'S THOUGHTS
> Because I don't know what the fuck I'm interviewing for and my life is falling apart.

> MARC
> I wanted to apologise. You're right, I ruined the night. I'm a twat.
> (beat)
> I'm sorry, I was out of control and got the bruise to pay for it.

Marc points to his fading black eye. Cara sighs, she looks away from Marc and out of the coffee shop window. She's annoyed at him but sympathetic.

                    CARA
     Look, I know you're going through a
     tough time at the moment with the
     firing and Spence leaving. I can
     appreciate you've got a lot on your
     mind.
          (beat)
     And... I'm not forgiving you, but I
     get it. We're good.
          (beat)
     But you're not getting away with
     it that easily, you still owe me
     that drink. Just, please be careful.
     Start looking after yourself.

                    MARC
     Yeah, working on it.
          (beat)
     Thank you.

                    CARA
          (Fully aware)
     That said, I know why I'm really
     here.

                    MARC
          (Coy)
     Why?

                    MARC'S THOUGHTS
     Of course she knows.

                    CARA
     Your interview is today? I'm not
     stupid Marc. I got you the inter
     view.

                    MARC
     No, I...

                    CARA

> (Interrupting)
> You're dressed in a suit and tie.
> It's before eight on a Thursday
> morning and I'm pretty sure you
> won't have any idea what the fuck
> you're interviewing for? Correct me
> if I'm wrong?

                    MARC'S THOUGHTS
> Ten out of ten, passed with flying
> colours. Am I really that predict
> able?

                          MARC
> Well...

                          CARA
>   (Interrupting)
> You're predictable, Marc.

Marc scoffs and sits back in his chair; he avoids eye contact
with Cara.

                          MARC
> Yeah, **of course** I know what I'm
> interviewing for. It's advertising,
> it's just fancy marketing with bill
> boards and poorly acted commercials.
> I'll be pitching ads, day drinking
> and business lunches with clientele.
> I've seen *Mad Men*, Cara.

Cara rolls her eyes and gives Marc an anguished look. She isn't
confident in him.

                    MARC'S THOUGHTS
> Fuck, I might actually want this
> job.

                          CARA
> You know it's just an entry level
> position, right? It's copywriting
> or content creation, something like
> that. You'll be starting at the **very**
> bottom.

>   MARC
>
> Yeah, I'll be fine. I'll just turn
> on the charm, advertise myself as
> somebody their company needs. Be
> somebody I'm not.
>
>   MARC'S THOUGHTS
>
> And then mentally check out after
> two months.
>
>   CARA
>
> Fucking hell Marc, take this ser
> iously. I had to pull strings to get
> you this interview.
>
>   MARC
>
> I know, I know. I'm just nervous.
> I'll get it all out now.

Marc checks his wristwatch. The time reads 7:54 AM. Marc's late
for his interview. He stands abruptly from the coffee table.

>   MARC
>
> Shit! I'm late. The interview's at
> eight.

Marc puts on his suit blazer and straightens his tie in the
reflection of the coffee shop window.

>   CARA
>
> Don't fuck it up.
>
>   MARC
>
> Thanks, again. We'll get that drink
> soon.
>
>   CARA
>   (Shy)
> That would be nice, I'd like that.

Marc stands and turns quickly from his chair toward the door
of the coffee shop. Upon his hurried turn for the door, he
collides into an ELDERLY CUSTOMER. The Elderly Customer is
holding two cups of coffee. The collision splashes black cof
fee onto Marc's white shirt.

Reeling from the heat of the coffee, Marc freezes and examines his shirt in horror.

> MARC
>
> FUCK.

TITLES OVER BLACK: MELANCHOLY DAYS

SFX: *Glass breaking and shattering.*

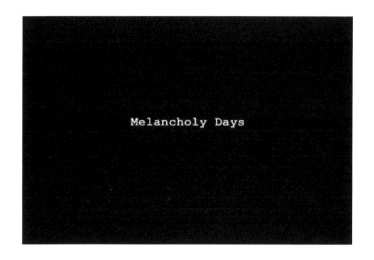

INT. COFFEE SHOP   MOMENTS LATER

Marc and the Elderly Customer are at a standstill, he's furious.

> ELDERLY CUSTOMER
>
> Now there is no need to swear young man. Didn't your mother teach you any manners?

Marc steps back from the Elderly Customer and assesses his shirt before glaring down at her.

> MARC
>
> What are you talking about? I don't think my language is really the issue here. Look at my shirt! Look what you've done.

Marc gestures towards the brown stain.

> ELDERLY CUSTOMER
>
> You should be more careful in fu
> ture. You young people are always in
> a rush.

> MARC
>
> Look, I don't have the time for this
> right now.

Marc attempts to shuffle by the Elderly Customer towards the door of the coffee shop. The Elderly Customer makes it diffi cult for Marc to pass. In his efforts to bypass her, he brushes against her leather handbag.

> ELDERLY CUSTOMER
>
> **Thief!** He's trying to steal my
> purse.

Marc holds both arms in the air to pledge his innocence.

> MARC
> (Shouting)
>
> What are you...?
> (beat)
> Definitely **not** trying to steal any
> body's purse. I'm late for an inter
> view, let me pass, please? I really
> need to go.

Cara watches from her seat in amusement. Marc finally manages to get around the Elderly Customer after several attempts.

> ELDERLY CUSTOMER
> (Shouting)
>
> **Thief! Adulterer!**

> MARC
>
> Adulterer? That's not even...

A male BARISTA approaches them with a real urgency to help. He's almost a little too willing to help.

> BARISTA
> (Interrupting, urgently)

> Is everything OK here guys? Is there anything I can do to help? Why not try our new *Caramel Matcha Hazelnut Roast Bean Latte* and hash this out as friends in our new outdoor social space?

MARC'S THOUGHTS

I'd rather drop a brick on my cock.

Marc turns toward the Barista.

MARC

All good here mate. Just a misunder standing...

ELDERLY CUSTOMER
(Interrupting)

He's trying to steal my purse! I think he tried to grab a handful whilst he was at it... **pervert!**

MARC'S THOUGHTS

No, I'd rather drop a brick on her. Dusty old hoover bag.

Marc furthers his disbelief at the situation unfolding before him.

MARC
(Panicked)

I didn't. I just need to get by, I have an interview to get to like... now?

BARISTA

OK, so that's a no to the *Caramel Matcha Hazelnut Roast Bean Latte*?

MARC
(Disbelief)

Are you even listening to me? Take a day off guy.

BARISTA
(Authoritatively)

I always listen to our customers.
> (beat)

I think you should leave sir.

                    MARC

I'm trying to. Believe me.

Marc begins for the coffee shop door at pace.

                    BARISTA

You should leave. Now. **Get out.**

                    MARC

As I've said, I'm trying to.

                    MARC'S THOUGHTS

What is with this guy? I'm wearing a
suit for fuck's sake.

                    ELDERLY CUSTOMER (O.S.)
> (Shouting)

Pervert!

                    MARC'S THOUGHTS

Just leave, you are doing fine. This
is fine.

EXT. COFFEE SHOP   CONTINUOUS

Marc exits the coffee shop and glances back down at the brown
stain on his shirt. He pulls over his blazer to cover the stain
and checks the time on his wristwatch.

The time reads 7:58 AM.

                    MARC

    Shit.

He sprints away from the coffee shop into the city centre.

EXT. CITY CENTRE   CONTINUOUS

Marc runs through the city centre to his interview. He hurtles
past people and avoids running into crowds. He arrives at Law
son's Media and Advertising, he's out of breath.

EXT. LAWSON'S MEDIA AND ADVERTISING OFFICE   MOMENTS LATER

Marc catches his breath outside of the exterior of the office building. He straightens his tie and tucks in his shirt. The building reads Lawson's Media and Advertising.

INT. OFFICE FOYER   MOMENTS LATER

Marc approaches the reception desk in the office foyer, he's moving at pace. As he approaches the desk, he pulls across his blazer to hide the stain on his shirt. The RECEPTIONIST ignores Marc's initial approach.

> MARC
>
> Good morning. I'm here for an inter
> view with...

He can't remember the interviewer's name.

> MARC'S THOUGHTS
>
> What was his name again?

> MARC
>
> ... Darren? At Eight?

> RECEPTIONIST
> (Looking at her screen)
>
> David?

> MARC
>
> Yes. David. Sorry, I'm a little
> late. You know how it is, traffic,
> the elderly...

> MARC'S THOUGHTS
>
> What?

The Receptionist glances up slowly from her screen towards Marc and scans him up and down.

> RECEPTIONIST
> (Bored)
>
> Name?

> MARC
> (Nervously)
>
> Pardon? Oh, sorry. Yeah, it's Matt.
> No, Marc. Sorry, it's Marc.

MARC'S THOUGHTS

Did I just forget my own name?

RECEPTIONIST

With a C, is it?

MARC

Yeah, that's me. Marc with a C.

MARC'S THOUGHTS

Seuss is spinning in his grave.

The Receptionist rolls her eyes.

RECEPTIONIST
(Robotic)

Second floor. Take a seat outside
the third door on the right.
(beat)
Also, you've got some brown on you.

She points to Marc's stain.

MARC'S THOUGHTS

Kill me.

MARC

Thank you so much for your help.

RECEPTIONIST

Yeah... you're late.

INT. INTERVIEW SEATING AREA   MOMENTS LATER

Marc walks over to the seating area and sits; he examines
the other interviewees. The interview seating area consists of
three chairs outside of an office. Two of the seats are already
occupied and Marc takes the only available empty seat in the
middle of the three.

INTERVIEWEE ONE is slender and pasty. He's slowly rocking back
and forth on the edge of his chair, he's very uncomfortable.
INTERVIEWEE TWO is older than Marc. She's dressed in a floral
suit and has matted dreadlocks with several facial piercings.

As Marc takes his seat, Interviewee One immediately stands from his chair.

> INTERVIEWEE ONE
> (Queasy)
> I can't do this. Not again. I'm
> going to be sick.

SFX: Dry heaving.

Interviewee One dry heaves twice before standing. He clasps his
mouth and sprints down the corridor away from the seating area.
He does not return.

> MARC'S THOUGHTS
> Was that me? Did I do that?

Marc and Interviewee Two both lean forward and watch Inter
viewee One leave. They both sit back in their chairs in
tandem. The atmosphere is awkward. Marc wants to diffuse the
awkwardness.

> MARC
> I don't normally have that impres
> sion on people... I swear.

> INTERVIEWEE TWO
> (Hopeful)
> No. This is good. I had an inkling
> something like this would happen.

> MARC'S THOUGHTS
> What the fuck?

> MARC
> I'm sorry?

> INTERVIEWEE TWO
> Pisces. My horoscope predicted this
> would happen today.
> (beat)
> I'm sure he was a Gemini, had to be.

> MARC
> Right. I get you.

> INTERVIEWEE TWO
> (Remembering)

'Others within a joint endeavour
will suffer as you continue your
journey alone.'

                    MARC'S THOUGHTS
So much suffering.

                    MARC
Ok... yeah.
          (beat)
Good luck with the interview.

Marc attempts to focus on the interview ahead.

                    INTERVIEWEE TWO
And you?

                    MARC
          (Distracted)
What?

                    INTERVIEWEE TWO
Your star sign... what is it?

                    MARC
Aquarius, I think? The one with the
song?

She cringes before issuing Marc a sympathetic smile.

                    INTERVIEWEE TWO
          (Confidently)
Oh dear, you sweet, sweet boy.
Well... best of luck to you. You're
going to need it.

                    MARC
Thanks... I think? What time is your
interview?

                    INTERVIEWEE TWO
10:30.

                    MARC
Why are you here so early?

                    INTERVIEWEE TWO
          Well, you see the shelter kicks us
          out early on a morning. Didn't have
          anywhere else to go.

                    MARC
               (Under breath)
          Makes sense.

                    INTERVIEWEE TWO
          I heard that.

Marc and Interviewee Two turn away from one another. Both sit
in silence for a moment.

SFX: Muffled shouting from within the office.

Marc brings his ear closer to the office door to hear DAVID
shouting from within.

                    DAVID (O.S.)
               (Shouting)
          Marc? With a C? Come. Now.

                    MARC'S THOUGHTS
          Thank God.

                    MARC
          Yes! Coming!

Marc stands, straightens his suit and tie before approaching
the office door.

                    INTERVIEWEE TWO
          Oh, you have some brown on you by
          the way. Very Aquarius.

Interviewee Two points towards his shirt. Marc glares back at
her with a grimace and enters David's office.

END OF ACT ONE

ACT TWO

INT. DAVID'S OFFICE   MOMENTS LATER

Marc enters David's office. The office is spacious, the walls are plastered with old print advertisements. David's desk is small and wooden and sits in the centre of the room. The contents of his desk include a desktop monitor, brown leather notepad (accompanied with a black pen), desk phone, face down picture frame and a dying spider plant. David is sitting look ing at his desktop screen. A single chair sits parallel to the desk for Marc.

Marc approaches slowly, David remains seated. In his late fifties and dressed in an outdated grey suit, David is the stereotypical businessman. The bags under his eyes cast a tired shadow as his disposition is expectedly cantankerous.

>   MARC
>   Do you want me to sit here?

Marc points towards the empty chair. David initially ignores him before lifting his head.

>   DAVID
>   (Bothered)
>   I'll be with you shortly.
>   (beat)
>   Well, are you going to sit or stand
>   gawking all morning?

>   MARC
>   Erm yeah, thank you.

Marc sits.

>   DAVID
>   Right, I'm here. Sorry about that.
>   So, it's Marc, right?

>   MARC
>   Yes, here for the interview... sir.

                    MARC'S THOUGHTS
Sir? Are we in a *Dickens* novel?

                    DAVID
Of course you are. So, I'm David
and I'll be taking you through the
interview this morning.

David leans over the desk to shake Marc's hand. David's
handshake is weak and slithery as both lock eyes during the ex
change. Marc retracts his hand quickly.

                    MARC'S THOUGHTS
Limper than a flaccid penis.

                    DAVID
Marc, let's start with an easy one.
Tell me a little bit about yourself?
I want to hear about previous work
experience, hobbies, any interests?

Marc is immediately uncomfortable.

                    MARC'S THOUGHTS
I'm a self loathing shower crier
with no hobbies and an alcohol
dependency.

                    MARC
Of course.
        (beat)
Yeah, a bit about me. Went the
standard route school, uni, drunk
for three years, graduated, post
graduate anxiety and stumbled into
an entry role in finance. Two years
of report writing, found my feet and
decided advertising was more my cup
of tea.
        (beat)
My hobbies include you know...
friends, sports and mountain biking?

                    MARC'S THOUGHTS
Mountain biking? Where did that come

from?

                    MARC
I'm just looking for a new challenge
really... something more my speed.

                    DAVID
And advertising is more your speed,
is it? Bit of a career change from
finance don't you think?

                    MARC
              (Backtracking)
You could say that. If we don't push
ourselves to try new things, then I
suppose we'll never truly grow into
who we're supposed to be.

               MARC'S THOUGHTS
Stop talking like that.

                    DAVID
                (Distant)
Yeah... I suppose so.
                (beat)
So, in terms of your previous roles,
do you have any experience in media
planning? Have you ever used any
tools to create an ad campaign in
any of your prior work experiences?

                    MARC
No... not really. I mean I've
eBay'd a few things online but it's
quite hard to advertise secondhand
CD's that nobody wants or uses...
does that count? No. I should just
stop talking. The answer is no,
I haven't. Finance was very number
based.

                    DAVID
At least you're honest.
                (beat)
Do you at least have a favourite ad

campaign from the last ten years?

>   MARC'S THOUGHTS

No.

>   MARC

Just Do It? Is that one? *Nike,* was it? Or when *Coke* put everyone's names on their bottles. I say that but I never did find a bottle with Marc spelt with a C. Yeah, probably *Just Do It* for me then.

>   DAVID
>   (Unconvinced)

Right. Sure.

David makes notes in his notepad.

>   DAVID

And Marc, why do you think this agency would be a good fit for you?

>   MARC'S THOUGHTS

It wouldn't.

Both pause. Marc struggles to answer.

>   DAVID

I'll phrase it differently. If you were to see an ad for yourself on line or on television, what would the content include? What would Marc the product be?

Marc pauses, he's caught off guard.

>   MARC
>   (Nervously)

Jesus. I think... well there would be me in the middle of it. I would probably be smiling. Fuck, I don't know man. Sorry, I swear when I'm nervous.

>   MARC'S THOUGHTS

Always nervous.

> DAVID
>
> Ok. We'll try something different.
> What keeps you motivated Marc? What
> gets you out of bed in the morning?

Marc pauses, he ponders the emptiness in his life.

> MARC
>
> To be honest with you David, I don't
> know.
> (beat)
> I don't know what gets me out of bed
> in the morning.

David allows Marc to elaborate.

> MARC
>
> I mean what else is there to do? You
> have to just wake up and get on with
> it, take each day as it comes. Every
> day.

Marc is having a moment.

> MARC
>
> You know, I wake up and tell myself
> that today is going to be better
> than yesterday or that today I'm
> going to make something of myself.
> That I'm going to find my feet in
> the world.
> (beat)
> It's hard to be that optimistic
> about life all the time. Each day
> feels like it's just another op
> portunity for me to make another
> detrimental life decision and with
> that comes even more worry about the
> day after that. Why take that risk?
> What's the point?
> (beat)
> You just have to carry on... keep
> waking up. You know, I...

SFX: Phone ringing.

Marc's moment is interrupted by David's phone ringing. David scrambles for his phone in his trouser pockets.

David's face erupts into anger as he brings the phone to his ear, he's outraged. He answers and again locks eyes with Marc who sits uncomfortably quiet as the call ensues.

> DAVID
> (Into phone)
>
> **WHAT THE FUCK DO YOU WANT, SHARON?**
> (beat)
> No, you can't have **my** records. You're hysterical, you know that? How fucking dare you?
> (beat)
> You've already taken everything else from me.
> (beat)
> Do you think this is what I need right now?
> (beat)
> Well, I'm fairly certain **Gavin** will have a record player for you. Or maybe he won't, he's only 22, right?
> (beat)
> Of course I'm going to say his fucking name... He used to be **our** personal trainer. Don't forget it was **me** who introduced you two.
> (beat)
> Oh fuck off.

David hangs up and breaks eye contact with Marc. He slams his phone onto the desk.

> MARC
> (Cautiously)
>
> Is everything... OK?

> DAVID
> (Aggravated)
>
> I'm sorry you had to see that. My wife fucked our personal trainer and

thinks I'm being unreasonable for
wanting to keep **my** *Genesis* records?

They both look at the picture frame face down on the desk.

> MARC
> (Uncomfortably)
>
> Breakups, am I right?

> DAVID
> (Unimpressed)
>
> We're getting divorced.

David looks into the distance beyond Marc before continuing the
interview.

> DAVID
>
> Anyway, your interview. Why are you
> interested in...

SFX: Phone ringing.

David snatches his phone from the table and brings it to his
ear. Marc braces for another uncomfortable call as David re
sumes furious eye contact with him.

> DAVID
> (Into phone)
>
> What do you not understand about
> **fuck off?**
> (beat)
> Don't you fucking dare touch *Peter
> Gabriel* until I'm home. I swear to
> God Sharon.

David hangs up and slams his phone back onto the desk before
breaking eye contact with Marc.

> MARC
> (Awkwardly)
>
> Shall I just...go?

> MARC'S THOUGHTS
>
> Now? Please?

Marc signals to the door behind him.

> DAVID
> (Seething)

I think that would be best.

Marc elevates from his chair quickly and looks down towards David.

> MARC

Thank you for your time this morn ing.

> DAVID
> (Flustered)

We'll be in touch if you're success ful by the end of next week.

> MARC

Ok. Sure.

> MARC'S THOUGHTS

Give him a second handshake? Fuck, maybe he'll rip it off this time?

Marc leans forward to shake David's hand.

> DAVID

Oh yeah, of course.

David leans forward towards Marc aggressively to shake his hand. As both lock hands, David again gives a weak and slithery handshake as he did at the beginning of the interview. Both are locked in eye contact, for the fourth time now.

Marc retracts his hand and accidentally winks at David. He turns and leaves for the office door immediately.

> MARC'S THOUGHTS

A wink? A fucking wink?
> (beat)

Leave now, before he clocks on. He might not have noticed. A fucking wink? Are you kidding me?

Marc opens the door and turns back to David.

> MARC'S THOUGHTS

Don't do it.

> MARC

Hope it all works out with Sharon.

David continues to stare back at Marc, he's very unimpressed.

> DAVID

Yeah, thanks.
> (beat)

Oh, and Marc... you have some brown on you. Looks like coffee or something? Not a great look for an interview.

David points down towards the stain on Marc's chest.

> MARC

Yep. Going now.

> MARC'S THOUGHTS

I hated this.

END OF ACT TWO

ACT THREE

EXT. CITY CENTRE   AFTERNOON

Marc walks through the city centre slowly. Still in his inter
view attire, he's avoiding going home.

He walks past the STREET PERFORMER from Episode One. The Street
Performer is knelt on one knee with his arms stretched out. The
city is busy, nobody is acknowledging his act. Marc stops and
watches him.

>   MARC
>   Why do you do it mate? Why this?
>   (beat)
>   What even is this? This can't just
>   be it?

The Street Performer acknowledges Marc but remains still.

>   MARC
>   Yeah, fair enough.

Marc begins to walk toward the tube station. The Street
Performer glances left and then right. He draws back his arms
to a natural position and glares toward Marc's turned back.

>   STREET PERFORMER (O.S.)
>   Need to do something.

Marc flinches, he's shocked to hear the Street Performer speak
for the first time. He turns and recoils back to him.

>   MARC
>   Fuck. Sorry. I didn't know you could
>   talk.

>   STREET PERFORMER
>   Look pal, I'm only going to say this
>   once. Life... it isn't linear.

>   MARC

What do you mean?

                    STREET PERFORMER
It's not always going to be good,
and you're not always going to get
what you want, but it's not always
going to be bad either. Life'll al
ways eventually regress back to the
mean, back to normal, back to the
middle.
          (beat)
You just have to keep going. Today
I'm back at that middle. It's
steady. Some days I'll make a kill
ing with this shit, other days I
make nothing, it always evens out.

The Street Performer resumes his act and outstretches his arms
whilst leaning on one knee.

                    MARC
Do you mind if I steal that from
you?
          (beat)
Why are you telling me this?

                    STREET PERFORMER
Because you needed to hear it.
          (beat)
And you look like shit.

                    MARC
Not going to fight you on that.

The Street Performer resumes ignoring Marc and looks beyond him
into the distance.

                    MARC
Thanks anyway.

Marc turns away from the Street Performer and begins for the
tube station.

                    STREET PERFORMER (O.S.)
You not even going to spare any
change? I still need to eat you

tight fuck.

EXT. THE TUBE STATION   EARLY EVENING

Marc arrives at the tube station entrance. He reaches for his phone from his trouser pocket. He reads his notifications.

> CARA (TEXT MESSAGE)
>
> *How did it go???x*

> SPENCE (TEXT MESSAGE)
>
> *Are you free tonight? We need to talk mate. Meet me at The Priory at 7?*

> MARC'S THOUGHTS
>
> Spence? Does he want to move back in? Sick of Mike already? Missing his floor bag? The broke brothers back in arms once again. As it should be.

Marc lifts his head from his phone. He smiles as he enters the tube station.

INT. THE PRIORY   EVENING

Marc enters The Priory and scans the room for SPENCE. He spots Spence sitting on a table in the corner of the pub and walks over confidently. The Priory is busy, loud.

> MARC
>
> Well, well. Here he is. Nice to see you mate, how've you been?

Spence lifts his head and looks up towards Marc from the table. There's an awkwardness about him, unrest.

> SPENCE
> (Awkwardly)
>
> Yeah, good man. How are you? Looking smart, what's the occasion?

> MARC
>
> Yeah good, cheers. Interview, a bit of a train wreck to be honest.

> SPENCE
>
> Sorry to hear that mate.

> MARC
>
> So... you needed to speak to me yeah? What's going on?

Spence avoids eye contact and looks into his empty pint glass.

> SPENCE
> (Awkwardly)
>
> Yeah. Got a few things I want to talk to you about.

> MARC'S THOUGHTS
>
> You've killed Mike and you want to move back in tonight?

> MARC
>
> Yeah man, of course. Fire away.

> SPENCE
>
> OK, so yeah you remember Cara's party? Well, I...

> MARC
> (Interrupting)
>
> Drink! What are you having? My round mate, same again? What is that? Cider?

> SPENCE
> (Uncomfortably)
>
> Erm, yeah it is.
> (beat)
> Marc, I really need to speak to you.

> MARC
> (Interrupting)
>
> Yeah, we have all night. Let me get us a drink in first. One second.

INT. THE PRIORY (BAR)   CONTINUOUS

Marc stands at the bar and attempts to get the attention of

the BARMAID. As he waits impatiently, David approaches the bar. David's already had a few to drink, his tie and hair are askew as he sways gently at the bar. He doesn't see Marc.

Both unaware of each other's presence at the bar, Marc notices David standing next to him first as they both fight for the at tention of the Barmaid.

> MARC'S THOUGHTS
> Fuck. Don't wink at him again.

> MARC
> (Politely)
> David?

> DAVID
> (Slurring)
> Marc, with a C? Is that right?

> MARC
> Yeah. You interviewed me this morn ing. Tell it to me straight, I bot tled it didn't I?

> DAVID
> (Slurring)
> You weren't awful. You were disap pointing, definitely disappointing, but not awful.

> MARC'S THOUGHTS
> Disappointing? Has he been speaking to Liv? Or Mum?

> MARC
> Yeah, people tend to say that about me.

> DAVID
> (Slurring)
> Look, now isn't the right time to be discussing the position but you did yourself a favour by not asking me about my pissing star sign.

> MARC'S THOUGHTS

Or steal your *Genesis* records.

                    MARC
I suppose that's something.

                    DAVID
                (Slurring)
I liked you Marc, you were honest
with me. If someone can sit through
a screaming match between me and
Sharon, then you might be someone
worth having around in the future.

David catches the attention of the Barmaid.

                    MARC
I **am** worth having around. You'll get
nothing but professionalism from me.
I wouldn't let you down David.

                MARC'S THOUGHTS
Just everybody else close to me.

The Barmaid approaches as David leans in to order his drink.

                    DAVID
                (Slurring)
Pint of bitter please love.

                    BARMAID
Is that everything?

                    DAVID
                (Slurring)
Yes, and whatever he's having...
he's paying.

David points towards Marc and smirks.

                    DAVID
                (Slurring)
You'll be hearing from me Marc...
with a C.
                (beat)
Piece of advice though... clean your
shirt... and don't get fucking mar

ried son.

David takes his drink and walks out of shot. Marc turns back to the Barmaid.

> MARC
>
> Yeah, I suppose I'll be getting his then. A pint of the cider and the IPA on tap... and a double house whiskey as well, please?

INT. THE PRIORY (TABLE)   MOMENTS LATER

Marc sits back down at the table and faces Spence. There's still an uncomfortable air between them.

> SPENCE
>
> Who was that?

> MARC
>
> That was David, he interviewed me this morning. Made me buy him his drink in exchange for the position, I think?

> SPENCE
>
> Or he's just taken you for a mug mate.

> MARC
> (Hopefully)
>
> Or that. Who knows? Feels like a step in the right direction for a change. Maybe I'm just clasping at straws. I don't know, don't want to read too far into it.

> SPENCE
> (Genuinely)
>
> I'm happy for you mate.

> MARC
>
> Before we go any further man I just wanted to apologise for the other night at Cara's. I was in a weird place with everything. You shouldn't

have seen that, it's been hard recently.

                    SPENCE
It's OK. That night, fucking hell, erm...

The colour drains from Spence's face.

                    MARC
Is everything ok?

                    SPENCE
              (Outrightly)
I slept with Liv.

Marc places his drink down on the table and is taken aback, he's speechless.

                    SPENCE
After you left, you know after Ben jamin hit you? I walked her home. We were both fucked after the party, it was late. It just...

                    MARC
         (Interrupting, genuinely)
It's OK mate. You don't need to explain.

He smiles forgivingly towards Spence.

                    SPENCE
Are you not angry with me? I'm so sorry Marc. I never meant for it to happen.

                    MARC'S THOUGHTS
Better, not bitter.

                    MARC
No, it's alright.
         (beat)
It's a shock... definitely a shock. I expected it from her, not so much from you mate but it's ok. We all

make mistakes. Life isn't linear, it's good and bad in the middle...

              SPENCE

What?

              MARC

I don't know. Heard it somewhere.

              SPENCE

It'll never happen again, I don't see her like that. I never have. It just happened, it was such a heavy night.

              MARC'S THOUGHTS

You're telling me.

              MARC

Don't worry about it man. Liv is Liv, she's great but her and I, we aren't anything. We had fun but it was over as soon as she brought Benjamin to the party. We're good here mate.
      (beat)
Move on and never talk about this again?

              SPENCE

Yes. Please?

Spence and Marc smile back at each other. Marc has finished his drink.

SFX: Phone ringing.

Spence ignores a phone call from MIKE.

              MARC

You not going to get that?

              SPENCE
      (Harassed)

No, it's Mike. He never leaves me alone.

> MARC'S THOUGHTS

Fuck you, Mike.

> MARC

Oh, really? Sounds quite... needy.

> SPENCE
> (Bothered)

I just don't want to watch *The Wire* with him every night, it's every single night. The guy has already watched it six times. I barely get any time to myself anymore.

Marc shares an uneasy look before glaring down towards his empty pint glass. Both pause.

> MARC

Well... I should probably get going.

Marc reaches for his suit jacket behind him.

> SPENCE

Oh, you sure? Everything OK?

> MARC

Yeah, of course. Long day, a pensioner accused me of grabbing her tit...

> SPENCE

Wait, what?

> MARC

Exactly.

> SPENCE

I'm going to hang back, I think. Mike's got *Find My Friends* on so he'll probably find his way here within the hour.

> MARC'S THOUGHTS

Fuck that for a laugh.

Marc stands from the table and looks down to a relieved Spence.

> MARC
>
> Take care of yourself mate. You've
> always got the bag at mine if you
> need it.
>
> SPENCE
>
> Thanks. See you soon, yeah?
>
> MARC
>
> Sure, see you mate. Have a good one.

Marc turns and heads for the pub exit.

EXT. THE PRIORY   MOMENTS LATER

Marc exits The Priory and walks out onto the road clenching his chest. He begins heavy breathing and stumbles towards the exterior of the pub for support. With one hand on the pub wall and the other on his chest, Marc is in the early stages of a panic attack.

The symptoms of the panic attack decline as he begins to control his breathing. He stands and looks onto the road ahead having successfully deflected a panic attack for the first time.

SFX: Door opening.

David can be heard stumbling out of The Priory. He's on the phone to Sharon.

> DAVID (O.S.)
> (Shouting into phone,
> slurring)
>
> I love you so, so, so much S Sharon.
> I'm so... so sorry. Take *Genesis*,
> take *Gabriel*, take me b back...

Marc smirks and carries on walking away from The Priory.

INT. BEDROOM   LATER THAT NIGHT

Marc sits down on his bed and begins to loosen his tie. He reaches into his trouser pocket for his phone.

> MARC'S THOUGHTS

Need to make amends. Got to make
things better with Heather.

He brings the phone towards his ear and the phone begins to
dial out.

SFX: Phone dialling out.

The call dials out once before being intercepted by the auto
matic voice of the dial tone.

AUTOMATED VOICE

This mobile number no longer exists.

Marc retracts his phone from his ear, HEATHER has blocked his
mobile number.

CUT TO BLACK.

END OF EPISODE FIVE

MELANCHOLY DAYS

Episode Six

ACT ONE

OVER BLACK.

SFX: *Muffled rush hour traffic and faint inaudible discussions between commuters fade in gradually.*

SFX: *Phone ringing.*

INT. BEDROOM   MORNING

The scene opens the same way the pilot did   MARC stands before his mirror examining his reflection. Much like the pilot, Marc is transfixed on his reflection in only his underwear. Some thing feels different about Marc.

Marc snaps from his trance, he's startled by his phone ringing.

>   MARC
>   Fuck. Shit.

CARA is calling, Marc answers.

>   MARC
>   (Into phone)
>   Yeah, what's up? You good?

>   CARA (V.O.)
>   Hey, yeah. Just checking we're still
>   on for later?

>   MARC
>   (Into phone)
>   Sure, just getting ready now. See
>   you soon.

>   CARA (V.O.)
>   Don't be late. I've got news.

Marc hangs up and throws his phone back onto his bed. He turns back to his reflection in the mirror. He smiles to himself, this is new.

> MARC

You're ok.

TITLES OVER BLACK: MELANCHOLY DAYS

SFX: Glass breaking and shattering.

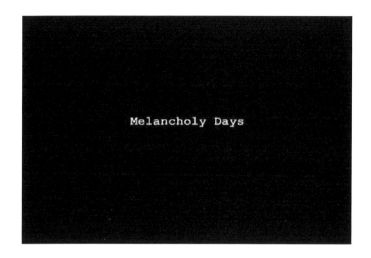

EXT. COFFEE SHOP (OUTDOOR SOCIAL SPACE)   LATER THAT MORNING

Marc and Cara are sitting having a coffee outside of the coffee shop from Episode Five. The sun is shining down on their table but there's a chill in the air.

> CARA

I'm surprised they let you back in after you nearly killed that pen sioner.

> MARC

I think it's more of a power play on my part for coming back.
> (beat)
Shows I'm not afraid of them.

> CARA
> (Confused)

Them?

                    MARC
You   know,   the   fucking...   head
grinders. The corporate chain.

Cara laughs into her coffee.

                    CARA
What the fuck are you talking about?
I think it's an independent.
          (beat)
You can be so... strange, Marc.

                MARC'S THOUGHTS
Is she... flirting with me?

                    MARC
Maybe. Anyway, what's new? How is
everything?
          (beat)
This *Caramel Matcha Hazelnut Roast
Bean Latte* is the tits. How are
you enjoying the new outdoor social
space?

                MARC'S THOUGHTS
That's it, move the conversation
along... I reckon I could work here.

                    CARA
          (Looking around)
It's OK, I guess?
          (beat)
Not a lot though really.
          (beat)
Oh! Shit! Yeah, my news, I forgot to
tell you. Sara promoted me.

                    MARC
Cara! That's brilliant, congratula
tions.
          (beat)
I'm **genuinely** so pleased for you.

She's puzzled by Marc's use of the word 'genuinely'.

                    MARC

It's... great news. You deserve it.
About time.

                MARC'S THOUGHTS

I can be genuine. I am a real
person.

                    CARA

It's a small pay rise. More of a
recruitment position for the com
pany than anything, a bit of hiring
and firing. Mainly bringing in fresh
meat for Sara to get her claws into.
        (beat)
Just means I'll be able to make Ben
jamin's life hell when starts next
week.

                    MARC

So, he got my job then?

                MARC'S THOUGHTS

And Liv.

                    CARA

He was the only one to interview.
If it's any consolation I don't
think he'll last long, you know what
Sara's like.

                    MARC

All too well.
        (beat)
You know she goes to group now?

                    CARA
        (Shocked)
What?

                    MARC

Yeah. It was like an out of body
experience seeing her there.

                    CARA

And then they fired you from there too?

                    MARC
Pretty much.

They both laugh it off.

                    CARA
Have you heard from David about the position yet?

                    MARC
          (Dissatisfied)
Nothing yet. I thought he might have had the decency to call already.

                    MARC'S THOUGHTS
But on the other hand, do I really want to take a phone call from him with his telephone etiquette?

                    CARA
I'm sure he'll call. Anyway, what's going on with you and Liv? I know you two...

                    MARC
          (Interrupting, seriously)
She slept with Spence.

Cara is aghast, she rests her coffee on the table.

                    CARA
What? No?

                    MARC
Yeah. After your party. Spence told me last week.
          (beat)
We haven't really spoken since.

                    CARA
Shit... and Benjamin?

                    MARC'S THOUGHTS

Still wants to kick my head in.

> MARC

No idea.

> CARA

Well... shit. Marriage pact if we're
both single at forty?

> MARC'S THOUGHTS

Is she flirting or friend zoning me?
Pick a damn lane.

> MARC

Sure, why not?

Cara sits forward and then reclines again into her chair; she can't focus.

> CARA

I can't get my head around this. I
didn't even know they were friends.

Marc zones out of the conversation and looks into the distance, he's deep in thought. He stands from his chair quickly and finishes his drink in one mouthful. He winces at the tempera ture of the coffee.

> MARC
> (Pained)

Fuck, that's still hot.

> CARA
> (Confused)

What the fuck are you doing?

> MARC

I've got to go. There's someone I
need to speak to.

> CARA

Is it Spence? Liv?
>   (beat)
Why is everything always so dramatic
with you? Grow up.

                    MARC
        Yeah, sorry. It's Spence.

Marc stands from his chair and walks out of shot. Cara's unhappy with Marc's immediate departure.

                    CARA
        Guess I'm paying then?

                    MARC (O.S.)
                (Walking away)
        What? Yeah? I still owe you. I haven't forgotten, thanks Cara!

                    CARA
                (Under breath)
        Two, you owe me **two** drinks.

EXT. PARK BENCH   LATER THAT MORNING

SPENCE is sat on a park bench opposite a water fountain in the nearby local park close to Marc's flat. The park is busy with families, a football match is underway behind the bench Spence is sat on. Mesmerised by the water fountain, Spence doesn't see Marc approach.

                    MARC
        Thought I might find you here.

                    SPENCE
                (Surprised)
        Fucking hell, how long was I staring into the fountain? How long have you been stood there? What are you doing here?

Spence acknowledges Marc and turns towards him from the fountain.

                    MARC
                (Coy)
        I was just... about, mate.

                    MARC'S THOUGHTS
        Are we playing hard to get? What's the game plan here?

                    SPENCE
        Do you want to sit? I'm just watch
        ing the fountain. Calms my nerves.

Marc sits beside him as they both investigate the water
fountain ahead. The atmosphere is awkward. Marc reaches for his
chest; he can feel it tightening.

                    MARC
        I'm just going to come out with it,
        I'm sorry Spence. For everything.

                    SPENCE
              (Almost instantly)
        I'm sorry too, mate.

They both share a look of understanding before turning back to
the fountain. A weight has been lifted as they collectively
share a sigh of relief.

                    MARC'S THOUGHTS
        Are we going to kiss?

                    MARC
        So... we good?

                    SPENCE
        Yeah, we're...

SFX: Ball hitting Marc's head.

Before Spence can finish his sentence, Marc is struck on the
back of his head with a football from the game behind. Marc is
knocked forward from the bench.

                    MARC
              (Shouting, pained)
        Fucking hell! What the fuck was
        that?

Marc caresses the back of his head and checks for blood.

Both turn and look behind the bench to see where the football
came from. They lock eyes with the FOOTBALL PLAYER responsible
for kicking the ball. He holds up his hand to signal an
apology.

                    FOOTBALL PLAYER (O.S.)
Sorry mate!

                    MARC
                (Aggravated)
Yeah, you will be. You fucking...
dick twat.

                    MARC'S THOUGHTS
Dick twat?

                    SPENCE
Dick twat? Doesn't seem...

                    MARC
                (Interrupting)
It's just a phrase, fuck's sake.

Marc turns back to the fountain and rubs the back of his head
whilst Spence kicks the ball back to the group before sitting
back down on the bench. Marc is agitated.

                    MARC
                (Agitated)
For fear of being hit by the pricks
behind us again, I'll just cut to it
mate... I came here to ask you to
move back into the flat.

                    SPENCE
Oh. Right.

                    MARC
We could upgrade the bag to a real
bed. No more sleeping on the floor.
Sound good, yeah?

                    SPENCE
I'll have to think it through. I'll
have all my things to move back in.
It'll take time.

                    MARC'S THOUGHTS
Two bongs, one sleeping bag and two
pairs of socks. A five minute job at

best.

                    SPENCE
And it'll be awkward with Mike.

                MARC'S THOUGHTS
Fuck you, Mike.

                    MARC
                (Confidently)
He's a big boy, he'll get over it.

                MARC'S THOUGHTS
Just like I never did.

                    MARC
Just think about it mate. It doesn't
need to happen immediately. As I
told you at the pub, you've always
got a place to stay at mine.

                    SPENCE
Will do. Oh, I meant to tell you. I
got the bank job from the interview
Mike sorted for me. The admin job
I told you about at Cara's party?
Meant to tell you about it at the
pub but didn't get the chance. I
start on Monday.
                (beat)
I'll finally be able to start paying
rent.

                MARC'S THOUGHTS
Two years too late. Could I backdate
his debt to me? No, stop thinking
about it.

                    MARC
That's brilliant mate. I'm **genuinely**
so pleased for you.

Like Cara, Spence is puzzled by the use of the word
'genuinely'.

                    SPENCE

Thanks... mate. Looks like it's all
coming together then, finally.
>   (beat)
Did you hear back from the bloke in
the pub yet? Darius, was it?

                    MARC
          (Downplaying it)
Oh, David? Nah, nothing yet. I
bought him a drink for fuck's sake,
he owes me this. Living in the city
unemployed is not cheap.

                    SPENCE
He'll call, don't stress.

                    MARC
I am stressed. I am **always** stressed.
It's probably why I feel like I'm
having a heart attack every time I
have a difficult conversation.

                    SPENCE
If I do move back in, you need to
promise to stop doing that self dep
recating thing in the mirror.

                    MARC
What self deprecating thing?

               MARC'S THOUGHTS
I know exactly what he means.

                    SPENCE
You know that thing where you stand
and look at yourself for twenty
minutes. You zone out a little and
then give yourself shit. It's **every**
morning.

Spence mimics Marc's routine.

                    MARC
If I agree, will you stop talking
about it?

                    MARC'S THOUGHTS
        And move in immediately after kill
        ing Mike with a hammer?

                    SPENCE
        Deal.

                    MARC
        Good.

                    MARC'S THOUGHTS
        Arsehole.

They shake hands in agreement and sit in peace for a moment.
This feels like a big step in their relationship.

SFX: Ball hitting Marc's head.

Marc is again struck on the back of the head with a football
from the game behind.

                    MARC
        FU...

END OF ACT ONE

ACT TWO

INT. BEDROOM   AFTERNOON

Feeling as though things are finally changing for the better, Marc begins cleaning away the empty whiskey bottles and lager cans into a black bin bag. He's moving with purpose and de termination. He opens his bay window curtains to let sunlight into the room.

Marc sets down the bin bag and picks up a full bottle of whiskey resting on his bedside table.

> MARC'S THOUGHTS
> Don't do it. Better, not bitter.

He considers drinking from the bottle before placing it into the bin bag after a moment of struggle. After his moment of weakness passes, he picks up the framed picture of himself and HEATHER. He inspects the frame before walking towards his window.

Marc pauses and embraces the warm sun pouring into the bedroom.

SFX: Phone ringing.

A withheld number is calling. Marc answers apprehensively.

> MARC
> (Into phone)
> Hello?

> DAVID (V.O.)
> Is that Marc? with a C?

> MARC
> (Into phone)
> Yeah. Speaking.

> DAVID (V.O.)
> It's David, from Lawson's Media and Advertising. Is now a good time to

talk?

Marc snaps to attention. This is the call he's been waiting for.

> MARC
> (Into phone)
> Shit. Of course. Yes. Thank you for getting back to me.

> DAVID (V.O.)
> Great. I just wanted to thank you for coming in and interviewing with us last week.

> MARC'S THOUGHTS
> The worst, most agonising seven minutes of my life.

> MARC
> (Into phone, profession ally)
> It's not a problem, thank you for having me.

> DAVID (V.O.)
> You're welcome. Look, I'm not going to pussyfoot any longer, I'd like to offer you the position Marc. How does that sound?

Marc falls back onto his bed.

> MARC
> (Into phone)
> Shit, **yes!** Absolutely. Thank you.

> DAVID (V.O.)
> Great. As I said, there's going to be a lot for us to work on and if we're being transparent with each other...

> MARC'S THOUGHTS
> Are we?

> DAVID (V.O.)

... your interview was terrible. But we can work with terrible. The role you'll be playing is a tad different to what you initially applied for. You'll be working under me as my go to guy. The pay's better and you wouldn't be starting at the bottom of the shit heap.
> (beat)

Does that sound like something you'd still be interested in?

> MARC
> (Into phone)

Definitely.

> DAVID (V.O.)

Fantastic. Let's say 9 AM, my office, on the 26th?

> MARC
> (Into phone, enthusiastically)

Definitely.

> MARC'S THOUGHTS

Stop saying definitely.

> DAVID (V.O.)

Great. Stop saying definitely and maybe tone it down with your enthusiasm on the day yeah? I don't want you to become a headache for me. I'll see you then.

> MARC
> (Into phone)

Of course. What do you want me to br...

DAVID hangs up.

SFX: *Dead phone line.*

Marc drops his phone onto his bed in relief and looks back down to the picture of Heather, he's still holding the frame. He rests the frame onto his bedside table and looks over to his suitcase in the corner of the room.

INT. MARC'S FLAT HALLWAY   LATER

SFX: *Doorbell ringing.*

Marc enters the hallway and approaches the door before squinting through the peephole at his visitor. LIV stands before Marc's front door crying, she's drunk.

SFX: *Banging on the door.*

> LIV (O.S.)
> (Hysterical, slurring)
> Marc! Can I come in? I need you!

> MARC'S THOUGHTS
> What does she want? To apologise?
> Harvest my organs for cig money
> maybe?

Marc stands cautiously behind his front door, he's hesitant to open it.

> MARC
> (Shouting through the
> door)
> Who is it?

> LIV (O.S.)
> (Slurring, aggressively)
> Fucking hell Marc, It's me! You
> should know my voice by now, you've
> fucked me enough.

> MARC
> (Shouting through the
> door)
> Shh Liv. The neighbours.
> (beat)
> Just had to be sure. Got a lot of
> people who want to kick my door
> down. Your boyfriend being at the

top of that list.

Marc reluctantly opens the door to Liv. Her make up is smudged from crying as she wipes the tears from her eyes. She enters the flat.

> LIV
> (Slurring)
> Ex boyfriend.

> MARC
> What do you want? Is everything OK?

> LIV
> (Slurring)
> Obviously not Marc, just look at me.
> I'm a m mess.

Liv barges past Marc and strolls into his bedroom. She eyes his bin bag.

INT. BEDROOM   CONTINUOUS

She slumps onto Marc's bed. Marc follows her into the bedroom.

> LIV
> (Slurring)
> You got anything to d drink? You've
> always got something.

Liv scans the room for booze.

> MARC
> (Sarcastically)
> Yeah, so would you like to come in?
> Please, take a seat.
> (beat)
> Oh, you already have.

Marc sarcastically points to the bed.

> LIV
> (Slurring)
> I need to s stay here tonight.
> (beat)
> Ben finished with me.

                    MARC

Benjamin.

                    LIV
                (Slurring)

I need you to look after me M Marc.

                    MARC'S THOUGHTS

I'd rather chew razors.

                    MARC

No, I can't Liv. We don't do that,
remember?

Liv spots his suitcase.

                    LIV
                (Slurring)

Where are you going?

                    MARC'S THOUGHTS

Anywhere that isn't here.

                    MARC

Just away, for a little while.

                    LIV
                (Slurring)

Please, Marc... d don't go. I don't
have anyone else. Have you found my
gear?

Marc perches on the end of the bed next to her.

                    MARC

I'm sorry, I can't. Not with you,
with whatever this was. I can't do
it anymore. You should go. We both
should.
                (beat)
I mean I need to go because I have
a train to catch but figuratively
we should both walk away from this.
Keep things civil.

                    MARC'S THOUGHTS

> Don't mention Spence, she doesn't
> need that. I don't need that.

Liv begins to come to the realisation that things aren't going to go her way.

> LIV
> (Slurring, angrily)
> No... y you don't get to end this. I
> do. **Fuck you**, Marc. I'm ending this,
> we're d done.

> MARC
> (Unbothered)
> That's OK. Look after your...

> LIV
> (Interrupting, slurring)
> You don't care. Why don't you care?
> You should care.

> MARC'S THOUGHTS
> Because you slept with my best mate.

> MARC
> I do, but I think we're good as
> friends. You'll be OK.

> LIV
> You're going to regret this Marc.

> MARC'S THOUGHTS
> Was that a threat? Toes in the post,
> a horse's head in my bed?

Liv stands abruptly and bounds for the bedroom door. Before leaving she steals the bottle of whiskey from inside the black bin bag. She exits his bedroom and then through the front door.

SFX: Front door slamming.

Marc remains sat on his bed, partly in shock at what's just happened but also happy in his decision.

EXT. HEATHER'S HOUSE   THE NEXT MORNING

SFX: Doorbell chime.

Marc stands on the footstep of Heather's front door. He's a man with purpose, with conviction. There's a chivalry about his demeanour.

SFX: Door opening.

HEATHER'S MUM answers the door, she's unimpressed to him.

> HEATHER'S MUM
>
> Twice in a month. That's almost as many times as you've seen her since it happened. Finally grown a con science have you Marc?

> MARC'S THOUGHTS

Should have left when I had the chance.

> MARC
> (With purpose)

I need to speak to Heather.

> HEATHER'S MUM
>
> If it were up to me, you'd be locked up.
> (beat)
> She doesn't want to see you, you should leave.

> MARC

I just need to explain...

> HEATHER (O.S.)
> (Interrupting)

Who is it?

Marc sways to the side of Heather's Mum to reveal himself in the doorway.

> MARC

It's me.

Heather rolls her eyes; she avoids eye contact with Marc. She's at the end of her tether with him.

> MARC

Can we talk? Please?

Heather's Mum shields her from Marc as she forms a barricade between them.

> HEATHER'S MUM
> I think it's best you leave.

> HEATHER
> No, Mum. It's fine, let him in.

INT. HEATHER'S BEDROOM   MOMENTS LATER

Marc sits on Heather's bed as she sits in her chair opposite him. Both are sat in the same places they were sat in Episode Four. The silence is tense, it's uncomfortable for them both.

> HEATHER
> (Annoyed)
> What are you doing here Marc?

> MARC
> I wanted to see you.
> (beat)
> I got a new job.

Heather is still unimpressed.

> HEATHER
> (Sarcastically)
> Congratulations, well done Marc.
> (beat)
> Have you come all this way to tell me that?
> (beat)
> Forgive me but I'm a little confused as to why you're here, it's weird. I told you not to come back here.

> MARC
> (Timidly)
> I'm trying to be better. Trying to fix things.

> HEATHER
> I'm glad to hear that but I don't

think you can fix this.

Heather gestures towards her chair.

> MARC
>
> It feels like I've been given a sec
> ond chance. Just what I need to...

> HEATHER
> (Interrupting, furiously)
>
> A second chance? **A second fucking
> chance**? At least you get a second
> chance, or a third, or a fourth
> Marc. When you leave here you get to
> get up, walk out of that door and
> go anywhere you want to without any
> restrictions.
> (beat)
> You can run away, walk, fuck, you
> could even crawl away if you wanted
> to, and you won't even think about
> how you did it. Or how grateful you
> are to have the use of your legs,
> how easy it is. A second chance...
> give me a **fucking** break. A second
> chance.

Heather laughs sarcastically as her eyes slowly fill with tears.

> MARC
>
> Heather, I didn't...

> HEATHER
> (Interrupting)
>
> **Don't**. Just don't... what don't you
> understand about leaving me alone?

Heather begins to sob quietly; she avoids eye contact with Marc. He's struggling for words.

> MARC
>
> No, I need to do this.

> HEATHER
> (Angrily)

Need to do what?
>   (beat)
Where were you when **I** needed you?
Where have you been when **I've** needed
you? This is only the third time
you've seen me since it happened.
It's been two years, Marc.

>   MARC
>   (Guiltily)
But I'm here now.

>   HEATHER
It's not good enough... I can't
begin to count the nights I've woken
to a missed call from you at God
knows what hour because you've drank
your guilt and you're feeling sorry
for yourself.
>   (beat)
The nights I've wept and shaken
because my PTSD has kept me from
breathing. The nights I've been un
able to move for fear of another
panic attack. I hate this.
>   (beat)
I hate **you**, Marc.

>   MARC
Heather, I didn't know you...

>   HEATHER
>   (Interrupting)
And why would you? You only ever
call or text when it's about you.

Marc reaches for his chest; he can feel it tightening. They're
both sobbing now.

>   MARC
>   (Sobbing)
I'm sorry.

>   HEATHER
I thought releasing you of your

guilt would have helped. Letting you go and freeing you of the hold I have over you. But it's not enough. It never will be.
        (beat)
I know what I need to do. I need to forgive you.
        (beat)
I need you to hear me when I tell you that I forgive you.

                    MARC
            (Sobbing)
Heather?

                    HEATHER
I forgive you, Marc. For all of it. I can see how much this is killing you.
        (beat)
We both need this.

Marc wipes the tears from his eyes.

                    HEATHER
I'll never look at this chair and not think of you Marc. It'll always be a reminder to me of what happen, how I got here.

                    MARC
            (Sobbing)
I need to help you. I can be there for you now.

                    HEATHER
No. You've done enough. We're not going to do this again.
        (beat)
It stops here.

Heather pauses and wipes the tears from her eyes. Marc sobs on the bed, he's inconceivable. She can truly see how broken he is as a person.

Heather wheels her chair over towards him and extends her arms around him. They both embrace knowing this will be the last time they see each other.

>   MARC
>   (Sobbing)
>   I'm so, so, sorry.

>   HEATHER
>   I know. I know you are.

SFX: *Knocking on bedroom door.*

>   HEATHER'S MUM (V.O.)
>   Heather it's time. You need to take
>   your tablets. Don't forget.

Heather and Marc retract from one another as their embrace comes to an end. Marc sits back onto the bed as Heather wheels backward slightly to give him space.

>   HEATHER
>   You should go. I need to take my
>   tablets.

>   MARC
>   Yeah. OK.

>   HEATHER
>   Be careful, Marc.

>   MARC
>   I'll try. I'll try to be better.

Marc stands and walks to the bedroom door. He wipes the tears from his eyes and turns to Heather. He glances back at her for the very last time.

>   HEATHER
>   You'll be OK Marc. You're moving on,
>   I'm **genuinely** happy for you.

Marc appreciates Heather's use of the word 'genuinely'. He gets it.

>   MARC
>   I love you.

He nods back towards her, rubs his eyes for a final time and exits the bedroom.

SFX: Door closing.

The shot cuts back to Heather as she continues to sob after Marc leaves. She brings her hands towards her face before glancing over to her bedside table.

We slowly zoom in on Heather's medication.

INT. TRAIN CARRIAGE   AFTERNOON

The shot cuts to Marc sitting on the train home. He rests his head on the carriage window. His face is tired from crying.

The shot slowly begins to zoom in on his face as he continues to look out the window of the carriage.

END OF ACT TWO

ACT THREE

EXT. THE COMMUNITY CENTRE   EVENING

Marc stands across the road from the community centre waiting
for the GROUP LEADER to arrive. He watches her park her car
before exiting the vehicle and unlocking the entrance of the
community centre.

> MARC'S THOUGHTS
>
> Be genuine, ask nicely, tell her the
> truth. Fuck, my heart is pounding.

Marc walks over to the Group Leader sheepishly before turning
back as if to walk away from the community centre. He tries to
avoid making any sound or being seen.

> GROUP LEADER (O.S.)
>
> Marc? Is that you?

> MARC'S THOUGHTS
>
> Rumbled.

He turns and faces her.

> MARC
>
> You got me.

> GROUP LEADER
>
> What are you doing here? Is every
> thing OK? It's nice to see you
> again.

He surrenders and walks towards her slowly.

> MARC
>
> Yeah, I'm getting by. I just wanted
> to...

> GROUP LEADER
> (Interrupting)
>
> I've been meaning to contact you. I

spoke to Mary, remember her?

                    MARC'S THOUGHTS
Snake in the grass.

                    MARC
          (Sarcastically)
How could I forget? My favourite
customer.
          (beat)
Sorry.

                    GROUP LEADER
Well, I don't know if it was the so
briety talking or a change of heart,
but she told me you didn't give her
anything that night.

                    MARC'S THOUGHTS
Only half true but I'll take it.

                    MARC
Oh, I see.

                    GROUP LEADER
I've been meaning to call you and
apologise, maybe ask you to come
back to group? I'm sorry for doubt
ing you, I hope you can forgive me
and come back to the sessions. You
were making great progress and we
would love to have you back with us
when you feel comfortable.

                    MARC
          (Excitedly)
I could come back tonight. I've got
nothing on.

                    GROUP LEADER
Excellent. Yes, of course. You could
come in now and help me set up
perhaps?

                    MARC

> Sure. It's cold out here anyway.

                    GROUP LEADER
> I really hope you weren't lurking
> out here in the shadows for me?

                    MARC'S THOUGHTS
> I was.

                    MARC
                    (Awkwardly)
> No, no. Just passing by.

Marc follows the Group Leader into the community centre.

INT. COMMUNITY CENTRE   MOMENTS LATER

We cut to shots of Marc and the Group Leader preparing the hall
for the night's session.

INT. COMMUNITY CENTRE   BEFORE THE SESSION

The community centre begins to fill with group members. SARA
enters and notices Marc. She waves awkwardly to him before
walking over.

                    MARC'S THOUGHTS
> Here we go.

                    SARA
                    (Awkwardly)
> You're back?

                    MARC
> In the flesh.

Both sense the awkwardness in the interaction. Sara looks down
towards her feet and then back up to Marc.

                    SARA
                    (Awkwardly)
> Well... I'm glad you're back. It's
> good to see you again Marc.

                    MARC'S THOUGHTS
> Hath Hell frozen over? Are we being
> nice to each other now?

                        (beat)
                Is she flirting with me?

                        MARC
                Thank you. It's nice to see you too.

                        SARA
                Thanks.

                        MARC'S THOUGHTS
                No, not everybody's flirting with
                you.

Sara smiles awkwardly.

                        MARC
                Thank you by the way.

                        SARA
                What for?

                        MARC
                Promoting Cara, she needed that. She
                works hard.

                        SARA
                She deserved it. Unlike you, she
                gets the job done. I'm going to put
                my...

Sara points to her jacket and then her chair. She leaves Marc
to find her seat in the room.

                        MARC'S THOUGHTS
                Marginally painless but still a dig.
                Are we friends? Don't be hysterical.

Marc finds a seat; he sits next to NEIL.

The Group Leader walks into the centre of the room and brings
her hands together to signal the beginning of the meeting. The
room falls silent.

SFX: Phone ringing.

Marc's phone begins to ring from within his trouser pocket.
Without looking at his phone, Marc declines the call and sig

nals an apology to the room.

> MARC
> (To the group)
> Sorry. Sorry everyone.

> GROUP LEADER
> It's OK. I think now is a good time
> to start the session.

The group nods and murmurs in agreement as the Group Leader finds her seat and sits down.

> GROUP LEADER
> It's hard enough admitting we have a
> problem but taking those next steps
> to seek help is even harder. I'm
> proud of all of you for making it
> here tonight. Coming to terms with
> our feelings and mental well being
> can be tough and that's why we're
> here to help and support each other
> through the darkness.
> (beat)
> There are no right or wrong answers
> in these sessions, we're here to
> listen and hopefully... heal our
> minds in the process.

> MARC'S THOUGHTS
> Here we go again.

> GROUP LEADER
> Before we go around the room, I just
> wanted to welcome back Marc. He's
> been away for a couple of weeks but
> we're happy to welcome him back this
> evening. Would you like to start us
> off this week Marc?

All eyes are on Marc. He reaches for his chest but doesn't feel any pain. He's composed and finally ready to talk.

> MARC
> (To the group)
> Hello, hi everyone. Thank you for

having me back here tonight.

INT. HEATHER'S BEDROOM   CONTINUOUS

Cut to Heather's bedroom. The camera slowly pans from Heather's bedroom door towards her bed.

> MARC (V.O.)
>
> As I'm sure you can probably tell I'm not great at talking about my self so I'm just going to start talking and hopefully stop at the end...

INT. COMMUNITY CENTRE   CONTINUOUS

Cut back to Marc.

> MARC
>
> ... sorry, this is hard.

> GROUP LEADER (O.S.)
>
> It's OK. Take your time.

> MARC
>
> Thanks. Ok, so, I was in an acci dent... it was about two years ago now. It was serious, a very serious accident. Somebody very close to me got hurt.

INT. HEATHER'S BEDROOM   CONTINUOUS

Cut to Heather's bedroom. The camera continues to slowly pan towards her bed. The camera passes her wheelchair, it's empty.

> MARC (V.O.)
>
> We were at a festival… I was out of control. My head had gone. I tried to leave because we needed more to drink, the group did... I should never have left.
> (beat)
> I lost control of the car, it flipped and we crashed.

INT. COMMUNITY CENTRE   CONTINUOUS

Cut back to Marc.

>   MARC
>
> She... she tried to stop me from
> leaving, to look after me. I should
> have listened, but I didn't, and she
> came with me.
>
>   GROUP LEADER (O.S.)
>
> Who, Marc?
>
>   MARC
>
> Heather, my girlfriend... ex, ex
> girlfriend.

INT. HEATHER'S BEDROOM   CONTINUOUS

Cut to Heather's bedroom. The camera continues to slowly pan towards her bed. The camera pans by her bedside table.

>   MARC (V.O.)
>
> She got hurt... really hurt. Worse
> than I did, I ran away, left her. To
> die.

Marc's voice begins to break.

The camera stops panning around Heather's bedroom. The camera fixes on a bottle of her medication. The bottle is overturned, it's empty. It begins to roll off Heather's bedside table.

INT. COMMUNITY CENTRE   CONTINUOUS

Cut back to Marc.

>   MARC
>
> The guilt is excruciating. The shame
> cripples me, the disgust I feel in
> myself. I'm the reason she can't
> walk. I did this, I couldn't stop
> myself. I couldn't save her.
>   (beat)
> I couldn't protect her. I was sup
> posed to be there for her, but I ran

away. Like a fucking coward.

INT. HEATHER'S BEDROOM   CONTINUOUS

Hard cut to a shot of Heather's right arm outstretched from her bed, her arm dangles over the side of her bed, lifeless.

> MARC (V.O.)
>
> I live with it every day. I drink to forget about it. I don't sleep, I can't function right anymore. I'm not a person.

INT. COMMUNITY CENTRE   CONTINUOUS

Cut back to Marc.

> MARC
>
> The guilt torments me, I'm tormented. I'm trying to get better.

INT. HEATHER'S BEDROOM   CONTINUOUS

Cut to Heather's bedroom. The empty medicine bottle falls onto her bedroom floor from her bedside table. Heather has overdosed.

> MARC (V.O.)
>
> I have to get better, for her. I owe it to her.
> (beat)
> To me.

INT. COMMUNITY CENTRE   CONTINUOUS

Cut back to Marc. Marc bows his head in relief he's finally opened up to the group. The room sits in silence. A weight has been lifted from his shoulders.

> GROUP LEADER
>
> Thank you, Marc. I know that must have been hard for you.

> MARC
>
> Just a little.

Marc lifts his head and nods back to the Group leader. It's

finally over.

A single tear rolls down his right cheek.

EXT. COMMUNITY CENTRE   LATER

Marc leaves the community centre and walks into the night alone. He remembers his missed call during the group session and reaches for his phone from his trouser pocket. He reads his notifications.

PHONE NOTIFICATION

One missed call from Heather.

PHONE NOTIFICATION

One voicemail from Heather.

CUT TO BLACK.

END OF SEASON ONE

Printed in Great Britain
by Amazon